"What are you doing here?" she asked, placing her hat on the stand by the door next to a top hat with ribbons she assumed was Abigail's.

"That's all you can say after all these years? No hug of welcome? Nothing more?" Abigail asked, her upper-crust British tones sounding odd to Mel's ears after years of Australian twang, as well as Alinta's pigeon English.

Mel smiled brittlely at her. She was filled with a strange mixture of feelings, both pleased to see Abigail looking so well, but not really thrilled to have her here in her home with her wife. "It's been a lot of years Abigail, or should I call you Lady Worthington?"

"You may call me Abigail, you know that," she said, feeling disappointed that Mel wasn't more welcoming or enthusiastic to see her. "My husband is dead. I'm now the Dowager Lady Worthington."

"I'm sorry to hear that. Your letter said you were interested in Australia, but I certainly never expected to see you here."

"You know why I'm here," she stated, looking at Mel meaningfully.

"No," she shook her head. "I don't. What are you doing here Abigail?"

"I'm here for you Meli …" she stopped herself, amending it back to 'Mel' before she could finish. "I came here to be with you."

Alinta, standing at the top of the stairs, listening, felt a clutch in her heart at those words.

Also by K'Anne Meinel:

Novels in Paperback:

SHIPS *CompanionSHIP, FriendSHIP, RelationSHIP*
Long Distance Romance
Children of Another Mother
Erotica
The Claim
Bikini's Are Dangerous
The Complete Series
Germanic
Malice Masterpieces 1
The First Five Books
Represented
Timed Romance
Malice Masterpieces 2
Books Six through Ten
The Journey Home
Out at the Inn
Shorts
Anthology Volume 1
Lawyered
Malice Masterpieces 3
Books Eleven through Fifteen
Blown Away
Blown Away
The Alternate Cover

Small Town Angel
Pirated Love
Doctored
Veil of Silence
Malice Masterpieces 4
Books Sixteen through Twenty
The Outsider
Pirated Heart
Recombinant Love
Survivors
Inn the Dog House
Flight
An Island Between Us
Malice Masterpieces 5
Books Twenty-One through Twenty-Five
Malice Masterpieces 6
Books Twenty-Six through Thirty
Beauty and the Beast

Vetted Series:
Vetted
Cavalcade (Prequel)
Pioneering (Prequel)
Vetted Further
Vetted Again

Novellas in Paperback:

Sapphic Surfer
Sapphic Cowgirl
Sapphic Cowboi
Sayyida
The Northwood Lodge

The Malice Series:
Mysterious Malice (Book 1)
Meticulous Malice (Book 2)
Mistaken Malice (Book 3)
Malicious Malice (Book 4)
Masterful Malice (Book 5)
Matrimonial Malice (Book 6)
Mourning Malice (Book 7)
Murderous Malice (Book 8)
Mental Malice (Book 9)
Menacing Malice (Book 10)
Minor Malice (Book 11)
Morally Malice (Book 12)
Morose Malice (Book 13)
Melancholy Malice (Book 14)

Mad Malice (Book 15)
Macabre Malice (Book 16)
Marinating Malice (Book 17)
Macerating Malice (Book 18)
Minacious Malice (Book 19)
Meddlesome Malice (Book 20)
Meandering Malice (Book 21)
Maniacal Malice (Book 22)
Monitoring Malice (Book 23)
Marked Malice (Book 24)
Mandating Malice (Book 25)
Methodical Malice (Book 26)
Malevolent Malice (Book 27)
Militarial Malice (Book 28)
Machiavellian Malice (Book 29)
Malefic Malice (Book 30)

Religious Experience
Lied

All Novels and Novellas in paperback are also available as e-books.

Novellas in Paperback Continued:

A Woman Down Under Series:
Shanghaied (Prequel)
Outback Born
Outback Bred
Outback Heritage
Outback Native
Outback Splendor
Outback Yearnings (Prequel)
Outback Escape

Pocket Paperbacks:
Mysterious Malice (Book 1)
Sapphic Surfer
Sapphic Cowgirl
Meticulous Malice (Book 2)
Mistaken Malice (Book 3)
Malicious Malice (Book 4)
Masterful Malice (Book 5)
Matrimonial Malice (Book 6)
Mourning Malice (Book 7)
Murderous Malice (Book 8)
Mental Malice (Book 9)
Menacing Malice (Book 10)
Minor Malice (Book 11)
Morally Malice (Book 12)
Morose Malice (Book 13)
Melancholy Malice (Book 14)
Mad Malice (Book 15)
Macabre Malice (Book 16)
Marinating Malice (Book 17)

In E-Book Format:
Short Stories
Fantasy
Wet & Wet Again
Family Night
Quickie ~ Against the Car
Quickie ~ Against the Wall
Quickie ~ Over the Couch
Mile High Club
Quickie ~ Under the Pier
Heel or Heal
Kiss
Family Night 2
Beach Dreams
Internet Dreamers
Snoggered
On the Parkway
Stable Affair
Kept
Stolen
Agitated
Love of my LIFE
Quickie in an Elevator,
GOING DOWN?
Into the Garden
The Book Case
The Other Women
Menage a WHAT?

LARGE Print Novels
SHIPS CompanionSHIP, FriendSHIP,
RelationSHIP
Erotica Volume 1
Long Distance Romance
Children of Another Mother
Bikini's Are Dangerous
The Complete Series
Malice Masterpieces
The First Five Books
To Love a Shooting Star
The Claim
Represented
Timed Romance

K'ANNE MEINEL

OUTBACK

FUTURE

ISBN-13: 978-1959436126

K'Anne Meinel is available for comments at KAnneMeinel@aim.com as well as on Facebook, Google +, or her blog @ http://kannemeinel.wordpress.com/ or on Twitter @ kannemeinelaim.com, or on her website @ www.kannemeinel.com if you would like to follow her to find out about stories and book's releases.

www.shadoepublishing.com

ShadoePublishing@gmail.com

Shadoe Publishing is a United States of America company

Cover by: K'Anne Meinel

OUTBACK FUTURE

PUBLISHER'S NOTE

This is a work of fiction. Names, characters, places, and incidents are the product of the author's imagination or are used fictitiously, and any resemblance to actual persons, living or dead, business establishments, events, or locales is entirely coincidental.

The publisher does not have any control over and does not assume any responsibility for author or third-party Web sites or their content.

CHAPTER ONE

"I want you, teach me those," she said in her pigeon English, indicating the firesticks that Mel had in abundance, one hanging above the door of the library and the others in the cabinet for their everyday use. Before, Mel had been the only one to handle them. Alinta always avoided them, but, after Bradley's second attack, she'd decided no man would ever touch her again. Not if she could help it.

Mel hesitated only briefly before nodding slightly, saddened that her wife felt the need to learn to defend herself with weapons. She knew she wouldn't always be about to protect her, a fact that had been proven. But she hoped, with Bradley's death, that was the end of that particular evil. She couldn't protect Alinta from everything, although she would try with her dying breath. Meanwhile, it only made sense to let her wife learn how to protect herself for those times that Mel wasn't about.

Mel showed her how to hold the gun, with the butt shoved firmly against her shoulder. Mel explained the things her father had taught her many years ago. Alinta dry-fired it many times, peering down the barrel at the sight on the end of it, and when Alinta felt comfortable with the weight of the long barrel, the heaviness of the steel, Mel began to show her how to load it, measuring out the gunpowder.

"It won't do you any good if the powder is too tightly packed. Don't let it *ever* get wet," Mel advised as she gently instructed Alinta.

The first shot startled the Aborigine woman, as it always did when Mel or one of the men used one of the firesticks. The recoil hurt her shoulder, but Mel advised her again to hold the stock tighter against her.

"No, don't close your eyes or you lose the target you just sighted. That will waste the gunpowder, and you know we'll have to wait for more to come from Sydney."

Alinta nodded. They were dependent upon too many of their supplies from Sydney to waste *any* of them. They grew what they could out here in the outback, but there were things they couldn't make or find out here like the gun and the powder, much less the shot, to waste it needlessly.

But Alinta knew Mel didn't mind teaching her, letting her practice, and using their precious supplies on that. She would have done it with her men, even their sons and any daughters that might take an interest. Already they had drawn several of the older boys and even girls, both white and Aborigine, as Mel taught her wife to fire the musket. She'd instructed all who wanted to learn how to clean, load, and even let them dry fire, but only Alinta was allowed to fire the gun because there were simply too many of them to let them practice actual shooting. As they learned over the coming days, several other women came and asked to be shown how to hold, load, and fire the guns, with their men watching on in

amusement until Mel glared at them. Despite being the station owner, none realized that Mel Lawrence was actually a woman, protecting her wife by teaching her to use the firearms proficiently.

"Any woman on this station who wants to learn to fire a gun, any child old enough, is welcome to learn," she told them and the men who had been amused hastily returned to work. Some agreed with Lawrence, realizing out here in the outback, the rules were different. Life was quite different, and their wives and daughters would have to be able to survive whether they were around or not. Some gave their permission for their wives to take the lessons, or even their daughters, and some forbade it. But those who refused to allow it were made miserable by their wives until some reluctantly gave in. Only a few held their ground, but they were looked on in contempt for denying their women the right to defend themselves or their homes if necessary.

"You're pulling to the right," Mel determined after Alinta finally stopped closing her eyes in anticipation of the blast. "It is too heavy for you?" she asked, challenging her wife.

"No, I get this," she answered, determined to learn how to shoot the long musket. She was pleased as she improved. Alinta's eyesight was far superior to anyone else on the station, being a native-born Aborigine, her senses were more in tune with nature and, once she got over her fears, she was deadly accurate.

As Mel taught her how to load and aim a handgun, she found she liked the shorter barrel and the lightness of the firearm better that the rifle, and many of the others agreed with her. Mel noted it was usually the women who probably didn't like the weight of the long barrels. Secretly she was pleased at their interest, but a handgun was no substitute for a rifle; it couldn't fire as far.

"If you find the gun too heavy, the barrel too long," she explained to her audience, showing them the various guns and their attributes, "you can use a branch or a stone to help you hold it steady. Never use your horse; you'll scare it something fierce."

Several women were pleased to find a tool to help, as these muskets *were* heavy, and Lawrence teaching them gave them confidence that they all could do it. The fact that Lawrence trusted his wife to fire the heavy, cumbersome gun made many of the women reevaluate learning it themselves. Even though they only dry-fired them, time and time again, they were certain they could shoot when necessary, and they certainly learned to load them correctly.

"You'll never need to use these with us men around," one boy boisterously assured a girl who had dry-fired the musket.

Mel glanced up to see who had spoken. She wanted to bite off the boy's head but kept herself in check. "What if the men aren't around?" she asked him reasonably. "Women can do anything a man can do," she told him, and, when his look turned slightly condescending, she let the girl he had been trying to impress aim and actually fire the musket she'd been practicing with. Her attempt was quite good.

"If we had more gunpowder for you to practice with, you'd be better than some of the men," Mel complimented the girl. She regarded the boy to see him flushed with embarrassment. "Don't let anyone keep you from learning something," she advised all the women and girls before turning back to the general discussion.

"It's important you keep your firearm clean." Mel showed them again how to clean the barrels of both the rifles and the handguns. "Keep your raingear over the firepan when it's raining if you want to keep your powder dry. You need that spark to fire the gun." The older children were

listening avidly, some of their mothers, too, concentrating on the lessons Mel was giving so freely to them all. The girls had grown less shy, now that they knew they had the station owner's approval. Seeing Mel teaching his wife made a few men reevaluate their reasons for not teaching their own women sooner.

Here was one of those things that confused Alinta. When Mel spoke of the rifle or the handgun, she called them both guns. She accepted it but thought that whites did this sort of thing deliberately to confuse others. She knew her people would be amazed if they could see her now. When her father had sought out white men to trade for their white man's stone, he had never considered or even known about the white man's firestick that could kill from afar. Its noise alone had kept him at bay. This tool, this gun, was much more valuable than just the white man's stone. It could kill from afar and give her time to hide or get away if need be, or if she missed. She quashed those memories of both her father and her people. Mel was her people now. Mel and Ainia.

"If you tie it like this, it won't interfere with your riding the horse." Mel showed them how to lash the scabbard to a saddle. She even gave Alinta a holster to keep at her waist, several of the youngsters looking on enviously when the station owner's wife was given a valuable gun, apparently to keep. "Remember, if you must shoot a boar ..." They had pretended she was learning to shoot in case of animal attack, but both of them knew it was in case of men like Bradley. "... kill it in one shot. You might not get a second shot." Mel glanced at her students, seeing the concern in several mother's eyes at the idea of a boar coming into the ranch yard. Mel kindly neglected to mention snakes, even though one had nearly gotten her.

There was another rifle, one that had two barrels, and Alinta tentatively learned to use that. The sight on it was odd, almost off-balanced, and she learned to move the barrels marginally to fire accurately. Even a small move on her part changed the trajectory of its bullet. When she felt confident enough with the different guns, she smiled warmly at her wife over the schooling she had received. She'd seen the longing on the older boys, and girls and the other women and wished they, too, could have shot. Most didn't even try the shotgun as they found the double-barrel to be too heavy.

"Don't ever point a gun at a man or a woman unless you fully intend to shoot and kill them. If you shoot to wound, they might come back at you at another time," she pointed out, exchanging a look with her wife. The dark, almost black eyes penetrated deeply into Mel's brown ones, almost to her soul. They understood each other, even if they never spoke of the rape.

The other women nodded sagely, and Mel heard the mutter from the men who had joined to help her instruct those who were learning, even if they didn't get to fire.

"Shore was a lot of shooting in that valley," a stockmen commented as he repaired a fence where a horse had kicked it down.

"Lawrence is teaching 'is missus how to shoot," Peter Winston, the ranch foreman, commented. He wrapped a rope he'd been using into a coil to hang up.

"Lord have mercy, a woman with a gun." The other man smirked, but the grin died on his lips when he saw the look on Peter's face.

"Don't let Lawrence hear you say that. He thinks mighty highly of his missus, he does," the man pointed out in warning. He knew how Mel felt

about his wife, and, while he didn't see the attraction to the Aborigine woman himself, a wife was sacred out here.

"Of course, he does," the man agreed readily, not willing to offend. The word had spread through the paddocks. Anyone with a disparaging word about Mrs. Lawrence was booted off the station. Mel Lawrence was too big and too ready with his fists to put up with such talk.

As they gossiped, Winston explained to the man who hadn't been there how Mel had taught any of the women who wanted to learn and several of the older youngsters, both boys and girls, how to handle, clean, and load the various guns. He hadn't let them fire them as they wouldn't waste the powder, but they were now knowledgeable.

"He teach the Aborgines too?"

"A few. Too many is scared of them fire sticks as they is callin' 'em."

"What's he planning, an army?"

"Nope, but no one better ever mess with Lawrence station," the foreman replied cryptically, and the man agreed.

Alinta felt better knowing how to use the guns but hoped she would never use them. She glanced at Mel who had taken off her stockmen's hat and was wearing a bandana to keep her hair back, the Aborigine woman appreciated how much her mate did for her, how much she respected her, and, while she didn't think of it in those terms, she knew she loved this big white woman, who looked so much like a man, more than life itself. She also knew that she, too, would kill to save Mel, as she knew Mel had eliminated that one threat for her.

CHAPTER TWO

As Mel headed for Menindee, she thought about what business she had there to accomplish. She could have sent one of her men, but she felt the need to get away from the home station for a while to think about her wife, her life, and what their future held. The many draws on her time were wearing on her, and she needed to see something else for a while, be alone for a time.

"Hellooo!" she called across the muddy river, getting the attention of the ferry operator, who eventually either saw her waving or heard her over the noise of the stream. She stared, fascinated, at the river which was so dirty, with endless swirls of silt and debris in its depths. She wouldn't want to drink from it. She watched as the ferry slowly make its way across on a cable that was strung across the river.

"Just you?" the operator called when he was a mere five feet from the shore.

"Yep, just me," she told him. "Are you new here?" she asked, trying to remember the man and failing.

"Aye, I am. Wilson took sick and I'm filling in for him until he gets better," he told her as the ferry, with a final helping heave from the river, slid up onto the shore. He opened the gate so Mel could lead her horse and pack horse onto the planks, closing it behind her. He lifted his rudder to push off from the shore, the ferry a little heavier with the horses' weight and having to wait until a wave helped him push the platform offshore. He quickly fixed the rudder into the apparatus that wove through the cable strung across the river and was thus able to control the speed of the ferry using the angle of the ferry with the rudder. "Come far?" he asked to make conversation. He enjoyed this job and liked meeting everyone coming and going across the river.

Mel nodded as she looked at the town, the dirty buildings weathering in the outback faster than anyplace she had ever seen. There was a new building going up, its wood bright and fresh against the backdrop of the other faded buildings, but Mel couldn't tell what it was going to be. "I'm from Lawrence Station," she told him. "I'm Mel Lawrence."

"Kin to the owner?" the man asked as he used the sweep to keep the ferry riding against its cable over the water. He could hear the odd accent the man had.

"I am the owner," she told him proudly. "Had some business here in Menindee and decided to take care of it myself."

The man nodded and then eyed the large man before him, completely unaware of Mel's true sex. He'd heard about this American who had brought in ten thousand merinos along with that other American who

owned part of another station he couldn't recall the name of. But he hadn't been at this job long enough to know everyone and everything. As they crossed, he chit-chatted about nothing in particular, not sure the American was listening to him except for getting an occasional nod. He watched when the man took off his stockman's hat to wipe at his forehead and stared at the bandana wrapped around the man's head. It was bright red!

Mel left off her hat to let the small breeze they garnered from riding across the river cool her sweaty brow. As they approached the other side, she asked the man, "Where will I find Wilson?"

"Wilson?" he asked in surprised before quickly pointing out the ferryman's house. After Mel paid him for the crossing, he watched as the American led his horses off the ferry and down the street, hoping he had done or said nothing wrong.

Mel knocked on the door of the house, and, when the woman answered, she asked respectfully, hat in hand, "I'm Mel Lawrence, is Mr. Wilson available?"

The woman's eyes opened wide at the American accent, but she quickly did a bob of a curtsy and waved him in. "He's in the parlor," she said, trying to sound a little posh but failing.

Mel saw the direction she had waved and headed into the room, feeling as though she were in her bathroom; the room was so small. The ferryman sat with his leg propped up on some pillows, smoking on a pipe and squinting at a newspaper. "Wilson?" she asked to confirm the man's identity, and he looked up in surprise, trying to rise out of respect for the station owner he recognized. Mel was familiar with him now, remembering him from previous trips to Menindee. "No, no, don't get up," she told him, waving him back to the settee. "I see your laid up."

"Aye," the man said, settling back down. He wouldn't have been able to get up, anyway. "Broke ma leg when a brumby lashed out and kicked me," he grumbled, sounding resentful.

Mel was amused but didn't show it. A horse's kick was nothing to fool with. "I want to talk some business with you if you're a mind to?"

Surprised, the man could only nod, and the only sign of his agitation was an increased puffing on his pipe. Mel liked the aroma of the tobacco and made a mental note to ask him what kind of fig he purchased. She'd tried many different kinds and had a few favorites of different flavor and smell. She wasn't always able to get what she wanted, as the drayage companies usually brought the cheapest items they could find and in large quantities.

"I'm Mel Lawrence," she stated.

"Aye, I recognize ye." He nodded for her to continue, and his mind turned to worry. Had his replacement man messed up something in the crossings? He couldn't afford to lose this job; he needed the income from the ferry to support his wife and children. He started to sweat.

"I'd like to set up an account for my station and pay you once a year, if that's all right with you?" she asked, coming to the point.

"Once a year you say?" the man mused, wondering if this would cost him. The money wasn't all his, after all. The ferry was owned by one of the paddleboat companies that came up this far, and he merely ran it for them, lowering the cable when they blasted their horn so they could cross. He heard one now and hoped his man lowered the cable in time or there would be hell to pay. He mentally shuddered at the thought of a cable getting caught up in the expensive and important paddle apparatus.

"If that isn't acceptable, I suppose we could pay the bill twice a year," Mel started, misunderstanding the intent of the man's question. It would

be a great convenience for the station as her supplies, any additional stock, or visitors rode the ferry across.

"Nay, nay, once a year would be fine for me, but I'll have to explain to the company ..." he left off, realizing he sounded weak.

"Yes, I understand that," she nodded. "You do that, and explain how much the drayage company takes to and from my station. It might not be worth it for smaller stations, but if it's a problem ..." she left off, leaving it hanging.

"I'm sure they'll agree, and I'll certainly let you know," he promised. They couldn't afford to offend these bigger stations. Lawrence Station, Twin Station, and others just as large were the reason they made any money, not the smaller stations or the day riders.

"Aye," she nodded, starting to sound like the Australian, "you do that. I hope you get better soon," she added, acknowledging his wrapped leg. She wondered briefly what Alinta would have done to help the leg heal. Whatever it was, she would probably have been more efficient, and it would have healed faster. "I'll let you rest then," she said, getting up from where she had sat. "Could you tell me where you buy your tobacco leaf?" she thought to ask. After he told her the shop here in town, a sound of surprise in the answer, she thanked him and then let herself out of the man's house.

Mel spent the afternoon exploring the small town, purchasing a few things she didn't really need including the new tobacco which she would buy in bulk for the station, talking to a few people, picked up their mail, but wondering why she had ridden all this way. It certainly wasn't to set up an account for the station with the ferry operator or her limited business in town. She speculated at her restlessness and thought about her wife, her daughter, and her station as she sat around her small fire that night, back

on her side of the river again, the ferryman apparently relieved to find he wasn't in any trouble. As she cut into a new fig of tobacco for her pipe, she thought over this peculiar restlessness that had been plaguing her for weeks now. Something needed to change. Perhaps it was bothering her to stay in one place for so long, something she hadn't done in years. Maybe it was something else; she didn't know.

As she headed back up the track towards home, she stopped to straighten the sign that pointed travelers towards Lawrence Station. The winds of the outback had faded the lettering so badly she took out some paint and touched it up. When she was done, she noticed how the other station signs had been added haphazardly below her own, many sparing only one nail for their efforts, which meant their signs frequently pointed the wrong way or even fell off from rough weather and wind.

Now absorbed in this project, Mel spent the day cutting down a tree and shaping it into a squared off piece of wood. She dug a deep hole in order to place the solid post into it. She attached the numerous signs on the tall post, with Lawrence Station at the top since it was the farthest that she knew of from any of these stations. She found it amusing how they had spelled their stations, some using family names, others using Aboriginal names or even landscapes to identify them. When she used stones to help sturdy the large post and straighten it into the hole, filling in the rest with dirt that she tamped down with her boots, she felt she'd done a good job. It looked impressive, and, with the half-dozen signs attached to it, it looked right. She did the same with the next sign and post she came across, as well as one more with only Lawrence Station and Twin Station on the last one. On each sign, she made sure the paint was bright and the post sturdy before she made her way back onto her own land and began to check on her stockmen, one by one, in each paddock until she

reached her home paddock. The weeks away had seemed too short but she was glad she had gone.

OUTBACK FUTURE

CHAPTER THREE

"**S**tart spreading the word to any of the swagmen you come across that Lawrence Station will be hiring for a time during lambing season. Any man or woman who wants to help our stockmen can hire on in exchange for cash money or supplies."

"I think the men will resent the interference, thinking you don't think they can do their job," Peters began, but Mel held up her hand to silence him. "And women? I've never heard of a woman tending sheep."

"That's just it; the men are doing their jobs until they are so tired they can't see straight. The swagmen want work, but only for a short time before they are on down the tracks. They don't want it permanent. Having extra men to help with the lambing when it's time, even with a jackaroo or two will help save lambs, which is to our benefit," she pointed out and watched as the dawning light of comprehension hit her head

stockman. She didn't answer his sexist remark since her own wife had helped out many times and, if he knew that Mel was actually a woman, he'd have been shocked.

"Aye, that's a right fine idea. Kinda like how they show up to help with the fires. A right fine notion," he mused as the idea caught hold in his brain. "I'll spread the word and have the men tell anyone that Lawrence Station is hiring for a time. This include the stockmen's wife? Extra pay for them?"

Mel wanted to point out it wouldn't be extra pay if the stockmen's wife was working, it would be her pay. However, she wouldn't debate it with her foreman as most men assumed anything a wife earned was theirs. She merely nodded at his questions. Mel smiled. The idea of hiring swagmen and the women that might accompany them as well as the wives of her own stockmen had occurred to her when she went to Menindee. Perhaps that was why she had gone on that trip; it certainly wasn't to straighten their sign posts.

She was pleased to see the fencing on their southern boundary was coming right along, if not painfully slow. It would take a long time, but she'd gladly paid the men their wages, knowing it would keep her sheep, any that got out of the folds they had built so long ago, from straying onto Twin Station land. Next, they would work on her eastern border, even though she hadn't even determined yet where her northern border was. Perhaps she should ride up there, too.

"May I go with you?" Alinta asked when Mel told her she would be gone again for a time.

"Are you sure you are up to the journey?" she asked, surprised.

Alinta had been depressed for so long, and Mel hadn't been sure how to snap her out of it. The learning of how to handle and fire guns had been a mere distraction, but the whole situation was one they couldn't really talk about. Mel hadn't touched Alinta since the incident, but that didn't mean she'd stopped wanting her. She was trying to be considerate, to give Alinta what she might want, but at the same time, the Aborigine woman was impossible to read.

Alinta was worried about Mel, too. She understood the distance between them to be somehow her own fault. Mel had needed to make that trip to Menindee to take care of business, but Alinta didn't really understand what business was. So, when Mel didn't ask her to go along with her, Alinta didn't know if it was her place to ask. She wished she had, but that was in the past, and now she was asking to go with Mel to inspect the station. She wouldn't beg, though.

Alinta had spent her time apart from Mel with Diablo, the young stallion, who welcomed her attention, especially when she began to feed the animal carrots and hay, befriending him. She had been surprised that an animal, one that would be food to her people, could show so many emotions. He was friendly, rambunctious, and playful. He was already causing trouble with Mel's herd stallion, who sensed a rival in the young, finely-bred stallion—and rightfully so. Since Mel wouldn't allow Diablo into the large valley behind the house, the young stallion was lonely and welcomed the woman with her treats and the cool water. He accepted her pats and scratches on his itchy coat and began to tolerate some light grooming. His coat would grow longer with the oncoming cold weather, and she was able to clear some matted sections on his mane and tail.

Ainia, strapped to Alinta's back, frequently reached out to touch the animal, her mother watching protectively.

Alinta had welcomed the time Mel took to teach her how to groom the rambunctious horse after Carmen had brought him to their station. Grooming him was soothing to the creature who could so easily have trampled the woman.

"I worry that the herd stallion will kill him if he gets out of this paddock," Mel told her, holding the bridle and petting the velvety nose of the mischievous young horse.

"Maybe he has his own wife?" Alinta had suggested. She loved the lengthening hairs on the horse, carefully saving the longer ones from the mane or tail as had been her habit for all of her life. She could weave them into practical things, but then she remembered; she didn't need the bags and such she would have made with these things. Even the spinifex she'd have used to weave baskets was cut down for the animals. Mel didn't discourage her from making these things, but she found the ones brought from Sydney to be of a much finer quality. Mel explained some of these things were made from machines. She didn't know what machines were but they made nice things. Still, she occasionally made her own because it comforted her to have her own things about her.

"That is a good idea. We can give him some mares of his own. You'll have to help me pick some from the herd," Mel offered, smiling at her wife for the idea. "We should build him a paddock of his own since we can't let him run in the valley with him," her chin indicated towards the valley where her herd stallion already held sway. "He'd challenge and hurt him if he could," she explained.

"Maybe Diablo hurt him?" she asserted, already feeling for the younger horse who was finding his way and wanting to defend him.

"I don't think he's big enough yet, but it would be a shame to let him get hurt. If we just let him run with mares on his own, he would want more mares and would eventually challenge the herd stallion for them."

Now, with Mel returned from Menindee and wishing to go on another ride, Alinta felt the need to go with her. She worried that Mel, like the stallion, would want more than one wife. In her own tribe she had known men who could afford to have two or three wives. Mel was very rich, in her eyes, and could easily have afforded as many wives as she wanted. Alinta had often wondered why this woman, who had the spirit of a man about her, had come into her life. She didn't quite understand it, but she accepted it and was grateful. She knew she didn't want to be put aside. She didn't understand love, but knew she didn't want to lose what she felt for Mel. It was all so complicated and confusing to the simple woman. She regretted that she hadn't been receptive to Mel's touches, normally making love with her frequently, but since the attack, that part of her was dead and she didn't know if it would come back. She was content with the cuddles Mel occasionally gave her, holding her close and safe in her arms at night as they slept. It had stopped the nightmares, at least for now.

Now, Mel had told her she wanted to go for a ride and Alinta's heart leapt as she asked if she might go with her. "Ride?" She looked to the mass of clouds on the horizon and could smell the rain on the breeze. It would rain soon and had been with increasing frequency. She would have to fetch her sheepskins, the ones that Mel had made for her that first rainy season with the sheep. As Alinta put away the grooming items she had used on Diablo, Mel explained.

"Yeah, Erickson was scouting about, looking for more places we could put a few folds to the north and discovered another valley. He says it's not as nice as ours," she gestured to the one behind the house. Their bedroom

overlooked the beautiful valley, and she loved waking up to look at it daily, catching glimpses of the stock they kept there, looking so wild and free. "I'd like to go up and check it out. Would you like to go with me? We could bring Ainia."

Alinta looked into Mel's brown eyes. She knew her wife was worried about her, but she couldn't—wouldn't—talk about the attack. It was in the past, and she wanted it to stay there. The memory would fade in time, and talking about it wouldn't solve any of their problems. She loved this big woman and knew Mel was trying to get back to the closeness they once had. They would once again make love, but she just hadn't been able to respond to the caresses—not yet. She wasn't ready. She would, however, please Mel in any way she could otherwise. If going to see this valley pleased her mate, Alinta would go with her, and it would be good to take Ainia. The little girl would love to be on horseback, riding with her mother and father. "Yes, we go. I will pack for us."

Mel smiled; she was pleased to get away with her little family. She turned to Erickson and said, "pick out some fresh horses for us to ride, and I'll get the gear."

The valley was much farther north than Mel had anticipated, and they ended up camping out two nights. Fortunately, the rain went farther south, hitting their southern paddocks, so they stayed warm and dry and the parched land and all the paddocks got the much-needed downpour.

Erickson was proud to show them this hidden valley, a bonus in an otherwise barren and desert-like region.

"I was following this game trail here," he indicated the path.

"Songtrail," Alinta murmured, but only Ainia heard her mother as she rode in front of her on the saddle. Mel was listening to her stockman and memorizing the way to the valley. With her wife and daughter along,

they'd gotten a late start the day before and so had to ride all day at a slower pace to finally arrive at the valley.

And it was a beautiful valley, with a stream running down one side of it and the other side having a cluster of tall trees full of birds, including pigeons, cockatoos, and other birds Mel hadn't learned the name of yet.

"If we close off that end," he indicated beyond the stand of trees, "this would make a perfect paddock for sheep, and we don't have to put up a fold, although I think the sheep would feel safer if we did."

Mel nodded to show she was listening, but she was thinking this would be better for a herd of horses and would solve the problem of having two viable stallions in close proximity. She could choose the mares that would go with Diablo, or maybe it would be better to move the older stallion that she hadn't named up here with his harem of mares since he was more experienced and could probably fend off any hunters on his harem.

"Let's look at the other end," she said agreeably, enjoying the stockmen's enthusiasm as she looked about the large valley. "Any signs of dingoes?"

"None that I've seen," the man admitted.

They saw no signs of the wild dogs as they toured the land, only spotting native animals like emus and wallabies were evident in the deep grasses. The birds made enough noise for everyone.

It turned out there was only one way into the beautiful valley. They found no other.

"I guess the way in is also the way out," Mel stated and Erickson agreed as they explored. "We won't need to close off that end," she indicated the cliffs. "Just put some bars across the rocks to keep them trapped in the valley."

Erickson worried about who would be assigned to oversee this remote valley. Some stockmen would enjoy being alone, but others needed to see people a little more often. He'd enjoyed exploring this vast wilderness for his employer, but didn't want to be tied down to one paddock.

Mel wasn't really worried as her plans began to take shape, thinking more about the horses instead of sheep. With a strong stallion, they could hold off any predators.

They made camp, and, after sharing a meal, Erickson slept on the other side of the fire, well away from the small family so they could have their privacy. Ainia was uncharacteristically tired after their long ride and running about in the grasses. Mel had played hide and seek in the grasses with her earlier, chasing and catching her in her arms, wearing her out in their play, as Alinta watched and laughed at their antics. Their daughter looked so happy, playing with the big woman. Alinta wished she could join in, but she was feeling ill, knowing the jerky hadn't settled right.

That night, as they lay on their bedrolls, Mel with her arm around Alinta protectively and Ainia on her own bed before them, Alinta felt Mel's caresses. When Mel would have stopped and pulled her arm back, Alinta grasped it and pulled it to her. She sensed Mel's surprise. As she drew the woman's hand down and slightly ground against it, the gasp behind her made her smile, and she turned to find Mel looking at her with longing and uncertainty.

Peering through the darkness, the fire not enough light to see Alinta's eyes, Mel tried to read her. Alinta captured the woman's lips, kissing her fervently, letting her know she wanted and needed her.

"Are you sure?" Mel had to ask when they came up for air as she started caressing more intimately, glad they were far enough from the fire, in the shadows on their side so that Erickson wouldn't see what they were doing.

"I want Mel," she admitted honestly.

"But …" she began. But Alinta silenced her with a kiss and reached for the trousers Mel had worn to sleep in, unbuttoning them to reach inside. "Ohhhh," Mel gasped into Alinta's mouth, trying to stay quiet, their child lying only a few feet away. Alinta found what she was seeking, the folds of flesh moistening beneath her fingertips.

Mel couldn't believe her wife was initiating this after so long, but she soon realized she shouldn't question a gift of this magnitude and quickly allowed her own hands free rein over her wife's supple body, slipping up the long shirt, surprised at the summer underwear she was wearing beneath it. Mel touched her all over, enjoying the feel of Alinta's body beneath her fingertips. After sufficient homage to the bountiful breasts, arousing her wife further, she quickly slipped inside the summer underwear to find the warmth between Alinta's legs.

It had been too long for both of them, and, between the caresses, the kisses, and now the determined application of their fingers, they both came quickly under the outback sky, smothering their moans of completion in each other's mouths as each panted deeply.

Mel finally pulled away, wondering if they had ever come this quickly before but not caring. Alinta had reached for her first, and the larger woman was thrilled.

Alinta had needed this closeness, not the thrusting of Mel's fingers, but the touch that made her body feel those delicious tingles. Mel would never hurt her and she had missed the feel of her body against her. She was

pleased that not only did Mel still want her after all she had been through, but that her body was coming back alive after all this time. She kissed her again and again in gratitude, vaguely able to see her in what firelight reached into the dark here.

Alinta hugged her close, tugged her own clothes back in order, and turned once again, pulling Mel's arm around her as she cuddled close to her *husband's* bulk. She looked towards Ainia, checking on the little girl who lay there so content. She reached out, pulling the blanket her daughter was laying on closer, and wrapped her arm around the small girl, and it was then that she felt movement for the first time, a tiny flutter inside of her, and knew Mel felt it, too, as she stiffened and sat up to look down on her wife. She peered at her in the darkness, trying to see her expression in the light from the fire.

"Did you …?" she began and then saw that Alinta had also felt the movement as she looked, at first shocked, then guilty, and then sad. "Are you pregnant?"

For the first time in her life Alinta wanted to tell an untruth, but she didn't know how. She nodded, wondering if Mel would be angry with her. She had started to suspect about a week ago but hadn't realized the consequences. To her amazement Mel's brown eyes, visible in a flicker of campfire looked at her with an unfathomable look.

"Are you happy to be having a baby?" Mel asked cautiously. Her own heart was beating hard with an anxiety she couldn't define.

Alinta didn't want to shake her head, but, remembering how the white people shrugged, she didn't want to do that, either. It was one of the odd things white people did. "I do not know," she admitted honestly.

"Because of how it was conceived?"

Alinta hadn't really thought about that. She knew now of course how Ainia had been conceived; she wasn't that naive anymore. But she hadn't thought about the fact that Bradley had beaten and raped her again could possibly result in a child. Her eyes grew huge as she thought of what Mel had just asked. Then, in that instant, she realized, Mel would never be able to give her a child of her own body. This would be their child, their last child. "I hadn't …" she began haltingly.

"If you don't want it, I know there are things you could take, but this would be ours …" Mel tried not to sound desperate or pleading, but now she worried, as Alinta had been depressed and quiet, too quiet, for a while. If Alinta took something, it might kill her too. Mel wanted the baby, and at the same time she wanted Alinta to be healthy and happy. She felt she had failed this amazing woman and wanted somehow to make it up to her. She was suddenly protective and uncertain, all at once.

Alinta had never thought of ending a pregnancy. She knew there were plants she could take, but she wasn't certain what ones they would be. Her knowledge of the native plants, especially in this area, didn't extend that far. She could probably figure it out since some plants were purgatives and with enough of them … no, she wouldn't do that. This was *her* child. Bradley had nothing to do with Ainia beyond her conception. This child, too, would be her child, and that man would never bother her again. Mel had seen to that. Mel, her husband-wife; she would protect her, protect them all if she could. She would be a father to this unknown child as she was to Ainia.

In a flash, she saw Mel playing with Ainia in the field earlier, catching her up and giggling with the little girl, and she knew that this child would be loved. This child would be wanted. She made a sign with her hand, and Mel saw it in the firelight. "This is *our* child," she said simply and

watched a smile spread across Mel's face. She had once thought it a grimace, the first times she saw that look on white people's faces until she realized it conveyed joy. She returned Mel's smile, realizing they would have another baby, and probably about the same time Ainia had been born several years ago, after the sheep dropped their lambs. Her hand went to her stomach where she had felt the movement, where Mel had felt the movement, and she shared a look with the American woman. They would be having another baby—*together*. She looked about the camp, recognizing the moment their child had come to life, when they had acknowledged that it was growing in her stomach. It was a magical moment for the two of them. She glanced down at their daughter sleeping next to her now. Ainia would soon have a brother or sister to love.

CHAPTER FOUR

Mel was especially solicitous of Alinta as they headed back early the next morning. "Are you sure you should be riding?" she asked, completely forgetting the fact that her wife had rode all during her previous pregnancy with Ainia. "Should I have Ainia on my horse?"

Ainia, hearing that, naturally wanted to ride with Mel, and Alinta handed her off willingly. The little girl was sick of riding and had been wiggly. Perhaps Mel could keep her in check. Ainia did behave and listened quietly as Mel and Erickson discussed the valley.

"We need to find a stockman who can handle horses. I want to use that valley for that stallion of ours."

"Maybe your older stallion," he suggested, confirming some of Mel's own thoughts. "He could keep off the predators who are sure to find the

valley, with more goings and comings through that." He pointed to where they had just come through the hidden entranceway.

Mel nodded, acknowledging that someone might know more than her. "We'll have to put a fence along that end to keep them from getting out," she mentioned, repeating the conversation from the previous day.

"Well, if you put horses here, that stallion can keep them, and there ain't enough grass up here," he indicated the rolling plains they were now on, "to keep a very large flock. Any stockman could check on the herd."

Mel agreed thoughtfully, envisioning it, and then a while later they found exactly where the permanent fold should go. Unsure if the billabong was lasting or fed from the springs in the valley, they staked out where the posts should go and discussed it. Alinta helped as they pounded in the stakes, watching with amusement as Mel held her horse by its reins with the toddler holding onto the pommel proudly, sure she was riding the horse all by herself. The little girl looked so pleased up on the saddle, her little dress shirt they had made for her spread out over her chubby legs, spread wide across the saddle as she held tightly on to the pommel. She looked proudly down at her parents as they worked, certain she was riding the horse all on her own.

"Okay, there's that chore done," Mel said while they pounded in the last stake. "We'll send a crew up here to make the fold and ask around for who would like the job," she said to Erickson when she helped Alinta up on her horse. Her hand lingered in affection on her wife's thigh as she looked up at her meaningfully, sharing a little smile of affection.

Alinta felt so good inside over her mate's love. She returned the smile and watched Mel mount up on her own horse, effortlessly controlling the animal when she got in the saddle behind their daughter. Her arms went around the toddler, firmly grasping the reins.

"Know any of the men who would like this position?" Mel asked Erickson, who shook his head thoughtfully. He didn't know a lot of the men at the home paddock too well. There had been new ones coming in, some hoping to get a job at the station. He spent a lot of time going to the outer paddocks and looking for possible new ones for Lawrence.

They discussed the new fold and valley as they rode. Mel was pleased with the find and gave Erickson full credit for it. As they discussed which of the horses they would choose to bring up here, Alinta was included in the conversation, voicing her opinion in agreement that the older and more experienced stallion would be a better choice to defend his mares against predators. She was secretly happy to keep the younger horse in the valley behind their home, enjoying the time she spent with the young stallion. She'd never had a relationship with an animal before in her life and was amazed at the things she was learning.

By the time they arrived back at the home paddock, things were pretty well decided. It hadn't seemed to take nearly as long to return to the home paddock, their plans and conversation made the time go by faster. When they were dismounting, Mel said to Erickson, "Gather a crew for tomorrow to go up there and build that fold. I'll have parts of a small flock brought up there. I think you are right; we shouldn't have a large one with that growth."

It would, of course, look different after the rains that were coming. Erickson could smell the rain even more strongly on the air. "I'll gather the tools and have them ready for first thing in the morning," the man agreed as they handed their mounts off to of the young grooms who ran up to take them.

Alinta took Ainia from Mel who was asleep in the woman's arms. "Better wake her so she can eat dinner and go to bed," Mel suggested with a grin.

"She mighty tuckered from the ride and your snacks," she teased her wife as she looked fondly down at their daughter. Mel had been sneaking crackers and homemade sweets from her saddlebags to feed the toddler as they rode, the adults only eating jerky to tide them over so they could be home well before dark.

"Whose are those?" Mel asked, spotting unfamiliar horses in one of the corrals.

Pete Winston came walking up. "Find something we can use?" he asked.

Mel turned to answer. "Aye, Erickson found us a right useful valley for a small flock, the extra horses, and one of the stallions. We staked out a fold near a billabong nearby. Erickson is loading up tools now, and I want you two to pick some of the men to go build it. Probably be best if Erickson goes up again, as he knows where it is." She saw the head stockmen stiffening up as she assigned some of his duties to another man. "I want you to trim one or two of the flocks that might be too big for some of the folds and send them up there. By the time you get a small-sized flock together, they should have the fold well along. Have the men going with Erickson and take all but a couple dozen of the younger mares and the herd stallion and put them in the valley he found. Ask for a volunteer, but it should be someone who likes to be alone." The man settled down, realizing that the boss was trusting him with choosing the sheep for this new fold as well as giving him his orders once again. Erickson wasn't taking his job. "Whose horses are those?" Mel repeated, nodding towards

the fine mounts including what were obviously some former Brumby's she saw in one of the corrals.

"Oh, you have some visitors. They are up in the house," he said offhand as he waited to be dismissed so he could help Erickson prepare for the trip.

Mel nodded to acknowledge him, now curious as to who was visiting their remote station. They didn't get company too often, and she glanced once again at the horses in the corral, wondering if they were from Twin Station, the only place they had gotten visitors in the past. Visitors normally stayed in the bunkhouse. "I'll talk to you tomorrow before you leave."

He nodded, hurrying off.

Mel took Alinta's outstretched hand. She had waited for her husband, and Mel now smiled down at her and the child still sleeping in her wife's arms.

Alinta looked around the busy station, the grooms removing their horses' saddles and children throwing scratch, a blend of feed to the grateful and greedy chickens in the pen. She could hear the ducks and geese down by the creek setting up an evening cacophony, with the cockatoos and other birds joining in. A horse neighed from the corrals, a cow answering it, and she could even hear the pigs grunting happily as someone fed them, too. Alinta was happy, this was her home, and, for the first time in her life, she understood the concept of home. She looked up at their house, the house Mel had built for them, and was beyond pleased to be there. She could forget the horrible thing that had happened in that house because her future was with Mel. She looked down again at their daughter, conscious of the life inside her that they would share, and she

wondered if she would have a boy child or another girl child. Either way, she looked forward to finding out. She was happy, very happy.

Mel felt the same way, almost as though she could read Alinta's mind, as she too looked about the place—at the lawns they now had, scorched from the hot summer's sun, yet kept trimmed by the youths assigned to it. She'd shocked a few people by allowing girls as well as boys to do the same work. She saw no reason they couldn't if they knew how to do the work. She wouldn't allow the younger children to touch a scythe, though, but they could feed the chickens, ducks, geese, and even the pigs, if they were careful. The place looked well kept: no weeds around the posts of the various corrals and pens, and even the rails on these were freshly painted and looked bright in the evening sky. God, she loved the outback! It was beautiful, and she grew to understood more and more, as Alinta had told her, she didn't own this land; it owned her. She walked with her wife and child up the steps, a cat arching as it stretched and yawned from where it had lain sleeping. She grinned at the lazy creature. They had lost only one of the kittens, and those that lived were doing the job she had hoped they would.

"Guess we can just put her to bed," Mel said softly as she glanced at their daughter and opened the door for Alinta.

"No wash?" Alinta asked, surprised because Mel was adamant about such things. She had thought of them as white man rituals, something she wanted for their daughter.

"Well, maybe …" she began but stopped talking as she saw their guest standing in the doorway of the sitting room.

"Hello, Melissa," the woman said and Mel stopped dead, staring at the incongruous view of Lady Abigail Baxter, she mentally corrected herself,

it was Lady Worthington now, standing there in her house in the outback of Australia.

"Abigail?" she asked, not sure she wasn't seeing things.

Alinta quietly observed the immaculately dressed woman standing in their home, and she immediately sensed this was not a good thing for her, for *them*. She looked to Mel to see what would happen.

"I go by Mel, now," she warned the woman, hoping that no one had overheard her or Abigail hadn't given away Mel's secret before they'd arrived. It was too important for people to think of her as Mel Lawrence out here instead of Melissa. Looking away, she saw that Abigail was staring directly at her wife. "This is my wife Alinta and our daughter Ainia."

Abigail stiffly nodded towards the Aborigine woman and didn't even glance at the toddler held in her arms before looking back at Mel.

Sensing that she didn't want to be around for whatever was about to happen, Alinta excused herself. "I take Ainia up." She said in a hushed tone and headed quickly for Ainia's room.

Both Mel and Abigail watched the woman dressed in an oversized man's shirt mount the stairs carrying the limp toddler. Mel turned to look at Abigail, noting she was dressed as befitted a noblewoman of her station. It looked totally out of place here in the outback, where they were much more casual in dress and manners. She looked older, more mature. Mel could feel the old attraction but was conflicted by it, as her wife climbed the stairs with their child.

"What are you doing here?" she asked, placing her hat on the stand by the door next to a top hat with ribbons she assumed was Abigail's.

"That's all you can say after all these years? No hug of welcome? Nothing more?" Abigail asked, her upper-crust British tones sounding odd

to Mel's ears after years of Australian twang, as well as Alinta's pigeon English.

Mel smiled brittlely at her. She was filled with a strange mixture of feelings, both pleased to see Abigail looking so well, but not really thrilled to have her here in her home with her wife. "It's been a lot of years Abigail, or should I call you Lady Worthington?"

"You may call me Abigail, you know that," she said, feeling disappointed that Mel wasn't more welcoming or enthusiastic to see her. "My husband is dead. I'm now the Dowager Lady Worthington."

"I'm sorry to hear that. Your letter said you were interested in Australia, but I certainly never expected to see you here."

"You know why I'm here," she stated, looking at Mel meaningfully.

"No," she shook her head. "I don't. What are you doing here Abigail?"

"I'm here for you Meli ..." she stopped herself, amending it back to 'Mel' before she could finish. "I came here to be with you."

Alinta, standing at the top of the stairs, listening, felt a clutch in her heart at those words.

CHAPTER FIVE

Mel directed the men as they hitched horses up to the wagon they would use to carry the tools up north to build the new paddock. She'd tried to think of the work involved, wishing she could go back with them and take Alinta and Ainia in order to avoid Abigail. She still couldn't believe the Englishwoman was here in the outback on her station, and she tried not to think of the reason she was here.

Alinta had given Mel the cold shoulder last night when she came to bed. The woman had decided to give Ainia a bath, after all, further tiring the toddler, who had fallen asleep, crabby, in the heat without any dinner. Alinta was in bed before Mel came upstairs, and she turned away as Mel got into bed. Mel, who already felt guilty over Abigail being in their home, as well as the woman's lofty assumption that she and Mel could just

pick up where they left off, thought she understood her wife's pique. She didn't realize that her wife was feeling insecure.

Alinta rubbed her stomach, hoping to feel the babe inside, trying to remember how good it had felt the previous night when Mel had expressed her desire not only for her, but for a child, *their* child.

Neither of them slept very well that night and Mel was up early to grab some breakfast and hurry out to her work; thereby avoiding her wife as well as her ex-lover.

Abigail hadn't slept any better than the couple had, despite the excellent bed she had been provided. It was certainly better than any of those they had been given on the trip out here and definitely beat sleeping on the cold, hard ground, as she had many nights. It was a lot more than she had come to expect, but, then, this station was a more established than she had anticipated after seeing the many other hodge-podge places that were merely functional. In fact, the many amenities in this house were surprising—running water, rich and polished wood paneling and cabinets, and modern furniture that showed refinement, yet were functional. It was, however, very hot, and she'd opened her window, surprised to find mosquito netting on the outside, which allowed the air in but kept the damnable bugs that had plagued her party the entire trip out of the room. Smart.

Melissa, or Mel—she corrected herself again—didn't seem pleased at all that she was here. This wasn't working out like she had planned. Mel hadn't welcomed her into her home, much less her arms; she wasn't dying to see her once again. And Alinta wasn't like anyone she had known before, but, then, she had stayed away so Abigail had only caught the one glimpse of her. She'd dismissed her simply because she was Aborigine. Surely Mel didn't want that simple woman when she could have Abigail.

She'd heard noise in the house in the early morning hours and got up to see Mel hurry out to the paddock, where they were loading a wagon and getting horses hooked up. She was dressed completely as a man, in fact, had Abigail not known differently, she herself would have assumed Mel was a man. She wondered at it.

The sheep station, too, was like nothing she had imagined. Those she had seen on the way out were not on the scale of Lawrence Station. She had thought the farms that Mr. Lawrence, Melissa's father, had bought and that eventually Worthington had acquired were good investments, but they were paltry in comparison to the size of the land Melissa had claimed. She had to consciously remember to call her Mel, as she'd been warned, knowing it would be devastating to Melissa if all these people who worked for her realized the deception that had been played on them. It also gave her immense power over Melissa if she chose to wield it, she thought contemplatively.

Dinner was awkward, Melissa—or rather Mel—apologizing that her wife wouldn't be joining them because their daughter had needed looking after. Abigail had looked puzzled until she realized that Mel actually thought of the child as her own. Realizing that Mel would never have children with her wife, she launched into an explanation about her own. Mel began to yawn halfway through her story about going to London to give birth to her twins and to escape her father.

"I'm sorry, but it's been a long day and this food has made me slee—py." She yawned, covering her mouth politely and stretching as she made her point. "My apologies. Could we pick this up tomorrow?" she asked as she made to get up from the dining table. She nodded immediately, letting Mel off the hook, and wished her a good night, but she harbored a

resentment that the American didn't seem to want to spend time with her. Was she avoiding her?

The next morning, Abigail called to her maid to help her dress in a riding costume, hoping that the curves it would reveal would catch Melissa's eye. She'd been surprised at the changes in her lover; her ideal of Melissa, based on the past she had shared with her, shattered. She'd known she'd grown up, but hadn't thought about Melissa maturing as well. She certainly hadn't anticipated the changes in her. She sipped her tea before the maid, with help from a washer woman, tightened the corset she insisted on wearing beneath her costume.

"Be careful, my lady. The heat here is something fierce," Brodie warned her unnecessarily. They'd just come through the bowels of hell to get here, so they both knew of the devastating heat in the outback. The maid observed that the lady they had come to see was not in attendance, and, although she wondered about it, she knew not to say anything because Abigail might take a comment as being impertinent.

"Thank you, I will," she stated, grabbing the matching umbrella in her gloved hands to ward off the intense heat. Before she could even use it, though, a raincloud rolled in, and the yard was soon drenched, Rivulets of muddy water emerged amongst the dead grasses. Not willing to go out into the rain and ruin her riding costume, she stood on the wide porch and bit her lip, peering out through the deluge until she saw Mel, who was organizing her men, and watching them leave in the wagon and on the horses. She didn't know where they'd gotten the extra horses, as she hadn't seen them in the paddocks when she arrived several days ago. But there were some fine ones in there, including a stallion. She decided to examine them further and made to get off the porch, but the rain stopped her again. She perked up when she saw Mel returning to the house.

"Good morning!" she said, bright and cheery, her face lighting up at Mel's appearance.

"It's a wet one," Mel said agreeably. She took off her hat to slap it against her thigh, and the rain fell from the brim onto the porch. Her clothes were drenched, but she was pleased to see the rains because the station was entirely too dry and desperately needed the moisture. "This is going to delay your return," she added, peering out at the torrent.

"My return?" Abigail asked stupidly. She had just gotten there!

"I assumed you would want to go back to Sydney as soon as possible, with this heat. Maybe back to England?" Mel asked, feeling her out and wondering what Abigail's plans were.

"I came all this way to see you," Abigail replied indignantly.

"I appreciate that—I really do—but a letter would have sufficed."

"A letter was not enough. I had to see you." Thinking of all she had gone through to get here: the travel by boat and across the immense continent that was Australia, just to get here only to have Melissa reject her—it was a bit humiliating. She was growing angrier by the second.

"That was a long and dangerous trip and completely unnecessary."

"Of course, it was necessary," she argued, wanting to stamp her foot in her mounting anger.

Mel just looked at her, knowing that Alinta was listening on the other side of that door. She'd seen her shadow beyond the mosquito netting, a very familiar shadow she would know anywhere. "What do you want from me Abigail?" she asked politely, resignedly.

"You," she answered promptly, fixing Mel with a look that would have melted her in the past.

Mel shook her head. "I'm happily married."

"But to a ..." she began, but Mel held up her hand.

"Whatever you were about to say, don't finish that statement. I love my wife very much. We have a child together and another on the way. If you came here under some misguided attempt to get me to go away with you, then you are in the wrong. You are welcome to stay until you are able to travel safely, once again, but I won't be putting aside my vows to Alinta. She's my *wife*," she emphasized, watching the English woman closely to see that she heard and understood exactly what she was saying.

Abigail was astounded. She had come so far to see Melissa, and it had never once occurred to her that the American wouldn't want her back. Her face flushed in her embarrassment.

Mel wasn't done, though, and, conscious that her wife was listening through the door, she continued, "As I said, you are welcome to stay, see our way of life out here, but then I expect you to go elsewhere. Back to Sydney or wherever. This is my life." She gestured at the station yard around them and then at the lands. "I've moved on Abigail, and I'm happy with my choices."

"But we were …"

"That was a lifetime ago," she was reminded firmly. "You made your choices back then. I've changed. This place has changed me, and I like what I've become."

"But if we were together you wouldn't have to dress like this or cut your hair or pretend to be a—"

"We will never be together again," she interrupted. "Please understand that. My life is here. There is no room for you in it except as a friend. I would hate to lose that friendship, as you were very significant to me at one time. My memory of that time is important, and I hope you won't ruin it by insisting that there is more now." She looked around, making sure no one else could hear them. The men had already drifted away in the yard,

seeking work that required them to stay inside the barns, the sheds, and not out in the wet paddocks. The wagon had gone on, with several men under a tarp used to cover the tools in the bed. The wagon driver and those on horseback were under rain ponchos and already drooping bush hats.

"I could tell everyone who you really are," Abigail stated haughtily, suddenly insulted that Melissa didn't want her.

Mel looked at her a moment. She heard, but knew the English woman could not, the slight shifting of Alinta's weight in the shadowed doorway through the screen. She knew Alinta understood more English than she let on at times, and she was probably angry at what she was hearing. Mel wasn't just talking to Abigail; she was talking so Alinta would know where she stood. That Alinta was her wife and Mel wasn't leaving her. "Yes, you could. No one would believe you, and I'd have to declare that your journey here had addled your senses, that you were mad. They'd take you away to be put in an asylum."

"You wouldn't do that to me," she gasped, her gloved hand going to her chest in alarm at the thought. That was something her father would have done to get his hands on her fortune.

"But you would do something equally reprehensible to get back at me?" she asked matter-of-factly.

Abigail hadn't thought of it like that. She'd just wanted to get to the safety of Melissa, to get far away from her father and his reach. She'd not thought about the changes that had occurred in the years they had been apart. She realized then, at that exact moment, she, too, had changed and wasn't attracted to Melissa in the way she had been as a younger woman. Deflated, her hands fell to her sides in defeat. "No, you are right. I wouldn't do that to you." She glanced around the beautiful porch they were standing on, talking as the rain fell off the eaves. Mel had made

something quite beautiful here. Even the barns with their dormers and gables had Mel's elegant touch. She closed her eyes briefly, realizing how much she had lost and how foolish she had been to come here. "But what am I to do now?"

Mel saw the defeat on her old friend's face, and it moved her. "Behave yourself," she teased and saw the old light return to those amazing violet eyes. She smiled until the English woman returned it. "Stay here. Learn what we do. You won't be able to travel comfortably for months, and there is a lot to see and learn about a station."

"Why can't I travel in this?" her gloved hand gestured out into the rain.

"Well, you could, but I thought you might be tired of traveling. What you did, coming to me through that," she gestured towards the outback, down the track they must have arrived on, "was extremely foolish and dangerous. I'm sure it wasn't easy." She stopped talking until Abigail nodded. "You need to rest for a while. I'm sure your children, your servants, and even your livestock do, as well. The rainy season isn't a good time to travel. Sometimes it washes out the roads. Otherwise, clear and dry washes become raging torrents. So, why inconvenience yourself further? Stay here for a while. See what we are building here."

"You raise horses?" she asked, having seen the young stallion in the paddock.

"Aye, we do, and we'll be raising more." Her chin nodded towards the herd that had just left. "I'm sending my herd stallion up with most of my mares to another valley."

"But why?" she asked, alarmed that Melissa would get rid of horses that way.

"It's hidden and has good grazing. I can't have two stallions. My new stallion, Diablo, young as he is, would fight my herd stallion, and I can't have that. He's a better stallion, but young, untried, and feisty."

"Is that the one I saw in the paddock?"

Mel nodded. "He's a fine one, he is," she answered, almost sounding Irish and jaunty. "My neighbor," her chin nodded towards the southwest, "brought his sire from California. She had a ranch there and inherited part of a station here and is raising some fine horses."

"I'd love to see what they have," Abigail put in enthusiastically before she even realized they were talking normally, with none of the tension she had created affecting their old easy familiarity. It was then that she realized that being Melissa's, now Mel's, friend was important to her. She stifled the feeling of disappoint within her breast. She'd come so far, and … she let that thought go. Melissa was not hers.

"Mama?" a voice said through the screen door, and Abigail jumped.

"Hello there, little one," Mel said, opening the door to let the girl out. She was much bigger than Mel had expected. She glanced into the room at Alinta, who nodded once, made eye contact with Mel, and then walked away, pleased with the conversation she had unabashedly eavesdropped on.

"Hello," the little girl said warily, looking up at the big man as she went to her mother. She hugged her mom's legs around her skirts since she couldn't reach Abigail's waist.

Abigail leaned down to pick her daughter up. "Mel …" she said, almost stumbling over the shortened version of Melissa and correcting herself before she could embarrass both of them, "this is my daughter Agatha. Lady Agatha Worthington," she finished, with all the snooty inflection of the English aristocracy in her voice.

Mel grinned, recognizing the cultured tones she had once known so well. "How do you do, Lady Agatha?" she asked, bowing slightly to the little girl.

Abigail smiled behind her daughter's head, realizing how much she had missed Melissa's humor. She turned to her daughter. "This is Mel Lawrence, our host here on the farm, er, station," she corrected herself. Her daughter stared at the man, and Abigail prompted her with amusement in her voice, "Say how do you do to Mr. Lawrence." The child smiled, thinking this was some kind of game.

"How do, Mr. Lawrence?" she lisped slightly and smiled before turning shyly into her mother's hair to hide her face.

Mel grinned. She wondered if Agatha—gawd what an awful name and probably Lord Worthington's influence—would be interested in playing with her own daughter, Ainia. With that in mind she called inside to the maid, "Betty?" Her voice echoed through the house, and soon footsteps could be heard on the second landing.

"Yes, sir?" she called back.

"Lady Agatha and Ms. Ainia should meet. The Worthington's will be staying with us for a while," she told the maid.

"I brought my own people," Abigail murmured, not wishing to impose on Mel's staff. "I had them keep my children away from everyone so they wouldn't be a bother."

"I'm sure they are worn out from the trip," Mel acknowledged again. "Let them rest, as you should, for a few more days. And the twins?" She hadn't seen the boys yet.

Abigail was pleased that Melissa remembered her sons. She hadn't realized that bringing them out here on that arduous trip could have killed them all. Their guide had warned them, but Augustus and Melbourne had

survived swimmingly, and she was pleased that Melissa would let them all stay. She had to warn Melissa that Melbourne was nicknamed Mel to avoid any confusion.

Mel and Ainia both met the young lords, Abigail explaining how she had obtained a lordship for the second son. When Abigail met Ainia, she was surprised at how white the young girl was. She looked at Melissa in wonderment. How in the world had Alinta been impregnated not once, but twice?

OUTBACK FUTURE

CHAPTER SIX

"You friend stay?" Alinta confirmed later after their guests had all retired.

It was a good thing they had so many bedrooms as the children and their maids needed two of the rooms and Lady Worthington her own. The other servants who had accompanied them could sleep in the basement or out in the bunkhouse.

"Yes, until the rainy season is over. I'm sorry, I should have asked you if you'd mind."

"Me?" she asked, confused. The rainy season had just started.

"This house is your domain," Mel answered, her hands spread to encompass the large house she'd built for her bride.

"I do not understand," she responded, confused. The tone of puzzlement was in her voice but also the look on her face.

Mel hesitantly drew her wife into her arms, pleased when she didn't pull away. "I built you this house to provide you with shelter and a home. I know your people don't look at things the way white people do …" she began, trying not to insult the woman she loved.

"I no longer them. I with Mel. My people are Mel's people now," she interjected, looking up at the big white woman and trying to understand. Mel had always been patient with her.

Looking down at the dusky-skinned beauty in her arms, she couldn't help but caress her wife's face, cupping her cheek as she explained, "The house is yours to do with as you wish. Those that stay here or don't stay here, that should be up to you."

Alinta tried to understand. Her people didn't have the same conceptualization of ownership that white people did. She'd always been surprised at the number of things white people traveled with. Things they had that she had no understanding of or need for. Even the clothes that were provided for her by Mel were vast riches beyond her understanding. She wore them because she thought Mel wanted her to. She kept Mel's house because she wanted to please her mate. Although the house hadn't been safe months ago, she did not feel it was Mel's fault in the least. After all, Mel was gone when it happened. Besides, that was all in the past, and Alinta wanted to firmly keep it there. She frowned as the thoughts bubbled up again as Mel held her. She liked the feel of Mel's strong arms about her body, the touch on her face warmed her from inside. The baby moved again, and they felt it between them. She smiled at the movement.

"I say no friend stay, no friend stay?" she asked, trying to understand the concept.

Mel frowned but nodded, hoping this wouldn't get awkward. How would she explain to Abigail and her entourage that they must go, and in

the rains? "Yes, that is your prerogative; your right," she agreed, "but I hope you will let her stay."

"Where she go?"

"That's just it; she would have to travel through the rains."

Alinta knew that white people didn't like to travel in the rainy season. Herself, a creature of the land, wouldn't have minded, but even her own people sought out caves or made huts of the surrounding brush to ward off the cold and rain in inclement weather. "I think they need stay," she stated and was rewarded with one of Mel's smiles.

"Thank you, my love," Mel said softly and leaned down to kiss her wife in gratitude. It had been a devilishly awkward twenty-four hours, and things could have gone much worse. She didn't know how she was going to get through the next months of Abigail staying here under the same roof as her pregnant wife, but maybe it wouldn't be so bad. Alinta approached things differently than white people did, and, although she tried to understand their ways, it didn't always work out. Sometimes Mel found it amusing, but this situation could still be difficult and Mel hoped to keep it from becoming that way.

Mel ordered the rams put in with the sheep to do their jobs so that the lambs would be born right after the rainy season. If the season went a little long, and had on occasion, they would be lambing in the rain, the cold possibly costing them many of their crop of lambs. It was a chance any rancher, any station owner, took in their constant gamble to raise animals in this God-forsaken country. After several years of this already, Mel knew what to expect and loved it all, good and bad.

Peter Winston, their head stockman, sent several men out to be sure that rams were let in among the ewes in every paddock. He sent along the monthly supplies that Lawrence Station provided their stockmen and jackaroos. He laughed when Mel still referred to jackaroos as cowboys, the American term for the job. "There ain't no cows among dem sheep," he said laconically.

Mel laughed along with him. "You're just tryin' to turn me into an Australian!" she accused.

They worked on the sheep folds and barns and got things prepared for spring, months in advance of when they would need the buildings. Alinta helped where she could, despite her expanding girth. Once Abigail saw that not only Mel's wife, but also the wives of the stockmen who lived at the home station, chipped in and were expected to work, she eschewed her London dresses, bought dungarees from the storekeeper, and started wearing men's shirts and an outback hat, a bushman's hat, to pitch in. She learned a lot from the men who always wanted to help teach her and talk to the pretty aristocrat, but she also learned a lot from observing the women who were willing, and able to do the work. Watching Mel work though amazed her, she did everything and tried her hand at things that Abigail didn't know she could do. No job intimidated the American woman.

Mel paused the first time she saw Abigail dressed as such. It hid none of the English woman's curves, and she looked quite fetching. Mel felt the old attraction but tamped it down. Sometimes she wondered what would have happened if Alinta wasn't in her life, but she stopped such thoughts quickly. She loved Alinta, and, seeing her rounding shape as she sustained the life inside, their child growing inside, it all brought home the life she lived out here. The life she loved.

"What kind of breeding went into that horse?" Abigail asked Mel, as they watched Alinta feed the young stallion treats. He seemed extra gentle with the woman, even rubbing his face along her stomach as though he knew what was growing inside her.

"I know that Carmen bred her Mustangs to a Hanoverian Belgian cross she had been raising. As a result, these are heavier, muscular horses. They are perfect for out here," she explained as she helped Alinta brush out Diablo.

"Why Diablo?" she asked, recognizing the Spanish word for devil.

Alinta smiled, her back to the English woman, knowing the story as Mel had explained it to her. Her people, too, had devils in their stories. She had loved hearing the stories when the families gathered each year.

"Carmen is of Spanish descent and her family well connected in Mexico. She lived in California, and her stallion Dancer breeds beautiful offspring," she emphasized her words with a slap to the rump of the rambunctious youngster, who was acting up now that Mel was close by. She had to stop thinking of him as being young; he was old enough to cover the mares she had kept for his harem. He was also decidedly interested in a couple of the horses Abigail had brought with her. She'd love to see what kind offspring the Thoroughbreds that Abigail owned would have from a crossing of these breeds. "Dancer is this one's sire. This one was starting to cause trouble on their station so she brought him along to trouble us," she finished with an affectionate smile as she looked at the fine stallion. She was so so pleased with him and that Carmen had brought him all the way from her station.

Abigail could hear the affection for the Hispanic woman in Mel's voice, but tried not to let the tiny curl of jealousy she could still feel develop into anything. She glanced back at Alinta who was enjoying the

stallion's antics as she backed away from him playing up, her hand protectively curved around her belly. Mel was married to this woman before her and while she had studied Alinta, she hadn't really spoken to her. She wasn't certain but the Aborigine might be avoiding her.

"I managed to convince her to let me have one of his offspring and he looks like he going to be a fine stallion," Mel went on.

"He plenty fine and plenty eager," Alinta put in, surprising them all that she spoke up. Diablo was nuzzling the her again, enjoying the caress she was giving his long and proud snout. He nudged her when she stopped for a moment, reminding her to continue.

"Oh, yes, I expect a good crop from him," Mel laughingly agreed.

"We should let him cover a couple of my mares," Abigail put in, surprising Mel further.

Mel looked up hopefully. "You'd lose a season?"

"Or gain a superior offspring. As your father said, it's good to get in new blood."

Mel was surprised again, but Abigail had been around a lot of horse people and Mel's own father had even listened to the young girl's advice on occasion. "Did you bring any with you to Australia?" she asked, having seen the fine Brumbies that had carried Abigail and her guards. At Abigail's nod, she asked, "How do you want to work out the offspring?" She wasn't willing to let the opportunity go.

"How about we see if he's any good and it takes?" Abigail asked sensibly, nodding towards the mares that were in the corral watching as they groomed the young stallion. "I'll send out a couple of my mares when we know his seed is good. Better yet, maybe you and I could raise horses together or work out some arrangement. After all, some of the horses I now own were yours at one time." She laughed.

Mel nodded, hoping to get a mare or several mares out of the deal so she could introduce the fine Thoroughbred bloodline into these horses out here. She knew a lot of the men rode Brumbies, the Australian equivalent of Mustangs, and who knew what breeds those were? A sturdy horse was desirable out here, and Carmen's horses were valuable, accordingly. The combination, though, of a Thoroughbred with those that Carmen was breeding might prove an interesting and even more valuable horse. She wondered how much Carmen would get for the many offspring she was breeding. She speculated selling some of her own but keeping many until she built up a large set of herds.

Mel watched the special connection between her wife and the young stallion. He had become her pet, but only because Alinta brought him treats. "Not too many of those," she had warned. "I don't want him to get a bellyache." But Alinta made sure to balance his treats with good food, plenty of water, and a fine bed, taking care of him when none of the men wanted to go near the fractious young horse. Only for her would he behave, although he tolerated Mel somewhat. He wasn't named Diablo for nothing and had terrorized the other men who worked about the pens. Mel had ordered that no children go near him out of concern for their safety.

Mel was pleased to let him cover the mares that had come into heat in close proximity to the virile stallion. He now had half a dozen mares of his own and protected them accordingly.

Used to having her men watch the stallions carefully when they covered her valuable mares, Abigail was surprised when Mel allowed the stallion in the delightfully beautiful valley behind their home, unfettered with the mares he had claimed. There was a pecking order, and the other horses would have to hold their own amongst the mixed Brumby mares that Mel was breeding the stallion to. Still, Abigail was surprised to see

Alinta slowly waddle out there twice a day, met on the path by the magnificent stallion to be fed treats or special feed and be pampered, brushed, or even just patted and praised. She didn't recognize the language the Aboriginal woman used, but she assumed it was her native tribe's. The woman was starting to fascinate her.

Abigail was also surprised that her older daughter was so drawn to Ainia. While younger than Agatha but older than Abigail's sons, she was just as tall as the English girl. She thought the outback must be responsible for her stature. Abigail herself was feeling good out here, eating heartily to the point her dresses grew tighter. Mentioning it to Mel during dinner one night, she was surprised when the American suggested she ride, despite the rain. "Or take a walk, like Alinta does. The air will do you good. Nothing worse than wet leather," Mel added. "Exercise comes unexpectedly out here."

Abigail was not surprised at that. It was amazing, the amount of work Mel did in a day. And, despite her pregnancy, the Alinta. Abigail still occasionally had a hard time reconciling the fact that Alinta was Mel's *wife*. Something she had never thought could occur between two women. The most she had hoped for was a companion.

"Just make sure someone knows where you may be going, and never go about without a gun," Mel advised.

At a confused look from Abigail Mel added, "this isn't England. We have wild pigs here that are fractious at best. Then there are snakes, so always wear boots. I hear there are spiders too that can kill."

"Why would you stay here?" she asked, gesturing at the vast home station that they were working on.

"I love it here," she said, glancing at her wife with with affection and then about the the place.

"When can you show me Twin Station? Aren't they just south of your own station?" She really wanted to see the horses that Carmen Pearson was rearing.

"Ah, that trip will have to wait until after shearing," Mel told her. "You don't understand that the sheep are going to be our focus for the next few months. Now, you could go back with the shearers. They could take you to Menindee and you could catch a paddleboat from there to get you back to Sydney." She herself had thought to take her there, despite the rain, but knew she was needed here on the station and could find no time.

"How far is Twin Station?" she asked instead, not sure if Mel was trying to get rid of her.

"About a week at moderate travel, but if you had a few horses and switched off, you could get there in a few days. Might kill you or the horse," she added as an afterthought.

Surprised and not thrilled at the concept, she decided to let that idea go. As much as she would have welcomed meeting the Hispanic woman who bred such fine horses, she would wait. There was still so much to do and see here at the home station. Mel had shown her some of the nearby paddocks, explaining how important sheep were, the different breeds they had brought in and why, pointing out the fine Merinos that dominated her flocks. "In a few years, I'd rather have almost all Merinos for the wool they bring us, but some of those," she pointed to Leicester sheep she had purchased a couple of years ago and then to the Poll Dorset and White Suffolk, "are good meat sheep. The Merinos are not only good for wool and meat, but, crossed with those, we have some great sheep."

"I'm familiar with the Leicester and Merino for wool," Abigail answered as they sat at dinner one night. She then told Mel about the wool mills Worthington had owned in Northern England.

"Wish you had one or two of them here in Australia. Everyone ships all their wool to England," Mel told her. "We have to wait months to hear if we're getting a wool check."

"I wouldn't be surprised if some of your wool has ended up in my mills." She laughed.

"What mill?" Alinta asked.

Used to her shortening of a question, Mel corrected her, trying not to make it condescending and then answered her. "What is a mill?" she repeated back correctly, knowing Alinta wouldn't make that mistake again. "It's a big building or buildings that have machines that turn the wool into cloth." She kept it simple because she didn't know the whole process herself.

"You might do well having a few people card and comb out some of your wool," Abigail stated.

"No room or time. Our job is to get them sheared and the wool off so they can take it by wagon to the ships to send to England. By then, we are dealing with lambing again and that's a nightmare time. I hope to hire more people this year, I put the word out before you got here."

"There aren't enough people to handle your flocks?"

"Some of these flocks are huge, and I myself have handled one by myself with just Alinta to help me, and with her largely pregnant," she confided, smiling at her wife as she remembered back. "She's worth a couple of jackaroos."

"Well, surely a few hundred sheep aren't going to ...."

"I think we had over four-thousand to handle that time, didn't we Alinta?" Mel cut her off as she looked proudly at her wife.

Alinta nodded, she couldn't count that high, not having learned the English words for it, but she understood the concept. She would agree to almost anything Mel said and then ask her later for clarification.

"You handled four-thousand sheep by yourselves?" Abigail asked, astounded. Although she hadn't been around a lot of sheep herself, she understood the concept, having owned some of the farms she had inherited. But there were others who kept them for her, and the sheepherders never discussed the grizzly details with a lady of her stature.

"That and more. They had twins and triples, even a few with four lambs, and we had to pull a few. Once they were done lambing, we had quite the flock. I think there was well over seven thousand or more. We split them up as we put stockmen on the various paddocks."

"How many do you have in a paddock?" she asked, realizing she hadn't understood the enormity, despite having seen the various paddocks and the masses of sheep. She helped herself to some of the delicious vegetables they had been served with their dinner. It was a roast, and she had enjoyed the flavor of the meat. She had been surprised how casual the meals were here at the station; none of the servants served their masters like in the grand homes of England. She wasn't sure if she preferred this to being waited on hand and foot, but there was something to be said for not having them watch everything you ate or listening to everything you discussed.

"Depends on the paddock. Some can graze more; some can graze less. Not every paddock is the same. The one we just set up north has very little grass, but that valley will be perfect for the horses and a smaller paddock for the sheep. There are other paddocks that have a stockman and one or two jackaroos to handle the larger flocks."

"And you aren't the only one who does this. I saw so many stations with sheep, and I just assumed ..." she left off, realizing how uneducated she had been about this side of the wool production.

"Being a grazer isn't all it's cracked up to be," Mel joked.

She and Alinta took Abigail along with them on a ride about the home station and to one of the near paddocks, laughing at her learning to ride astride, unfamiliar with the muscles used and ones the Englishwoman would be feeling later.

They rode along slowly since she didn't want to spook the sheep. It was a fine winter day, and they were all dressed warmly in wool coats, Mel having lent one to the Countess since her London coats were inadequate. Riding astride in dungarees would take getting used to. It was actually quite scandalous to find her nether regions in contact through the fabric of the dungarees on the leather, but Abigail found she preferred it to riding side-saddle as she had been expected to back in England. There was so much freedom here.

"Dingo," Alinta murmured to Mel, pointing with her chin as she reached for her rifle.

Abigail watched in consternation as her American friend leapt into action, untying her own rifle from her saddle as she kicked her horse to give chase on the dog-like animals. She was equally surprised when the Alinta, despite her pregnancy, steered her own horse in a wide circle away from Mel to head off the wild dogs. Still not understanding what was happening, she watched as Mel unlimbered her rifle, shot, and waited a second for the smoke to clear before aiming and firing again. This was

followed by two shots from Alinta's rifle, giving Mel time to reload, despite being on the back of a running horse. By the time they were done, seven shots had been fired and six of the dogs were dead or dying. Mel primed her misfired barrel and shot at point blank range to kill a dying dog.

The stockman came riding hard. "Mr. Lawrence, you okay?" he asked, concerned, and then looked about at the dead dingoes. "These must have just moved in," he said in excuse and then flushed in guilt. It was his responsibility to make sure that dingoes were killed in his paddock, not stalking and killing the sheep that Lawrence paid him to guard.

"Hang them, gut them out, and you leave the sheep with your jackaroo. I want them wiped out of here before they can get too established," she ordered the man sternly. She reloaded her gun, watching as Alinta finished reloading hers. "I expect more than these for your efforts." At his nod, she looked at him hard for a moment, and she turned away, followed by Alinta, to join Abigail, where they'd left her to watch them obliterate the pack of dingoes.

"Can't let those things get established or they'll wipe out an entire flock," she explained to the English woman. Glancing at her wife, she saw a face softened from the stern expression she had been wearing. "You did good," she complemented her.

"You fire good, too. Miss only one," Alinta replied.

"That's because this misfired. I hope those guns I ordered from America come in soon."

"It's getting late. We should turn back now," Mel stated. They all started their horses back towards the station house. Mel looked hard at the horizon, trying to see if any storm clouds were there to signal another storm coming in.

"You ordered guns from America?" Abigail asked, curious.

"Yeah, these things are ancient," she patted the musket as she replaced it in the boot, making sure to tie it down. "They have repeating rifles that fire a bullet, and I'd much rather have those. Eventually those will replace these," she patted the musket again to emphasize her statement. "They're hard to come by out here, but I placed a substantial order a couple of years ago and another one later, knowing that shipping them here is fraught with danger and theft. I suspect my first order has been stolen, as it hasn't arrived."

"Well, hopefully you'll get the second, but what will you use for ammunition?"

"We can make our own, from what I learned," she told the Englishwoman, knowing that Alinta wouldn't ask such questions but was listening avidly. "I also sent away for the fixin's." She went on to tell of her time in America, punching cows, and how she wound up in San Francisco.

After a while, wanting to include Alinta, Abigail asked her, "You said there was a dingo, and yet you both killed six?"

Surprised to be addressed, Alinta tried to explain, "Dingo no travel alone. Pack, family. I circle while Mel start them runnin'."

Abigail understood more now and nodded thoughtfully as they rode back towards the home paddock.

It was the last clear day for a while, and Mel was off supervising the men who were felling trees and hauling them back to the station to be sawed into boards for various uses. Alinta had saddled up, intending to

ride a little, when Abigail asked to go with her. Surprised, she nodded and then watched as the Englishwoman saddled up one of the horses left for anyone's use. The Brumbies she had brought with her were down in the valley.

They rode southeast along the track, not saying a word. Abigail let Alinta take the lead, and they walked the horses slowly, probably due to the Alinta's pregnancy. They both could hear the chopping of wood in one of the many forests about the station.

The rain was coming down in a lighter mist, it was why Mel felt the men could work today. A downpour would not have been good for them to be cutting wood, the blade and the wet would have been miserable work for the men. They could both hear the sound of axes against the dull sound of the wood they were striking, echoing across the quiet valley. They rode across the creek that had a fair amount of water in it, over the bridge that Mel had built a few years back and up the far side of the valley.

As the silence stretched between them, Abigail was unsure of what to say to the woman. Should she apologize? For her part, Alinta made no attempt to start a conversation, but, then, Abigail had noticed she rarely spoke to anyone except for Mel.

They took a track that bisected the main one and headed west, paralleling the creek. Abigail watched the other Aboriginal people, the ones that had a village on this side of the creek. Mel had explained to her that many of them worked for her for wages. They looked very different from Alinta, but they were of different tribes, or so Mel had told her. Mel had also explained they spoke a different language than Alinta so everyone had to try to use English to communicate or make signs. Abigail had been surprised that Alinta and the other Aboriginals didn't speak the same language until Mel compared it simply to English versus Scottish.

Abigail saw Alinta rub her stomach a couple of times and wondered if the babe was kicking, remembering her own pregnancies and comparing them to Alinta's. No one would have let her near a horse, and, yet, Mel encouraged Alinta to get out and exercise. When Abigail had mentioned it wasn't good for a pregnant woman to ride, she scoffed at the idea.

"Alinta is the healthiest woman you ever want to meet. She doesn't gallop, she rarely runs a horse, and she needs to get out and get fresh air. If it wasn't the rainy season, she'd have Ainia up on the saddle before her."

Mel had explained about naming her daughter after the Amazon woman who fought the Greek god Achilles, but when Abigail had worked up the courage to ask who the father was of the babes, she had shut down. "I'm their father," she stated bluntly and left it at that. Abigail hadn't had the nerve to ask again. Although she was still curious, she knew it was none of her business. She did wonder how it had come about.

As they began to climb a hill again, they saw someone trotting a horse along a track that was about to intersect with their own. Both of them marginally sped up their horses to meet up with the rider.

"Howdy," the man said, doffing his hat, despite the mist, out of respect to the women. His glance darted between the Aboriginal woman and the white woman. "I'm looking for Mel Lawrence?"

"I, Alinta Lawrence, Mr. Mel wife," Alinta stated in her pigeon English.

The man removed his hat again quickly. "Beg your pardon, missus. I have a couple of letters here from Twin Station for Mr. Lawrence."

"I take them," she stated, and he quickly reached in a saddlebag behind him to reach in and fish out the waxed leather case and hand it to her. "You go up to bunkhouse, get some tucker?" she asked him kindly.

"Yes, ma'am. I'll do that. Thank you," he answered respectfully, putting his hat back on his now wet hair and pulling at the brim respectfully. He nodded to the white woman with the owner and applied heels to his horse to hurry it along.

That was a lot of words for Alinta to have spoken, and Abigail was impressed. Without bragging, she had told the man who she was, and a hint of pride was in the word *wife*. With that, a piece of the puzzle that was this enigmatic woman fit into place for Abigail. This was Mel's wife, her mate, her partner for life. They could live openly here in the outback, and, while they may have fooled some people back in Sydney, as well, no one here seemed to notice that Mel was actually a woman. Her appearance, her demeanor, everything about her made people assume she was a man. This woman accepted all of that and took her place as his wife. Abigail could never have been Mel's wife in that way. Aside from that, she didn't know if she could live in this isolation. While Lawrence Station had many amenities to make it pleasant, the people were simple, and there was no outside stimulation. The library was extensive, but, eventually, all the books would be read, and there would be nothing else except for hard work for them to do. Abigail didn't mind hard work, but just the amount they had told her was coming defied her imagination. She couldn't imagine it; she had to see it. That meant staying here indefinitely. She knew she wanted more than Mel could ever give her, now. She wasn't sure what it was that she was seeking, but it wasn't this. She couldn't live out here. Unlike her, this woman she was riding with was uniquely suited to the life Mel had chosen out here in the outback.

They continued their ride in companionable silence, heading back to the station house, where the young men being trained as grooms ran out to take their horses and return them to the barn. The rain began to come

down harder, and the sounds of axes stopped out in the forest. Alinta and Abigail took off their boots before walking into the house on stockinged feet. They did not leave the boots outside, though, instead leaving them inside the door on a carpet the maid had left for that purpose. Abigail had been warned never to put on boots outside here without first banging them together to make sure nothing had tried to make a home in them. After Mel's warning she didn't ask what those things could be, she simply didn't want to <u>know.</u>

As Alinta headed for the library to leave Mel the wrapped packet, Abigail made her way upstairs to change. The dungarees, man's shirt, and wool coat were too much to wear anywhere but on the back of a horse. She preferred her dresses when she went about the house. She visited with her young sons, enjoying their toddling about the room they were using that was a nursery. They still shared the crib that they had found there, Ainia's old crib. The maid who watched these two was relieved to leave them in their mother's care while she ran to get some lunch. Abigail didn't mind; she was going to make sure she was a better parent than Worthington and his nasty housekeeper would have allowed her to be for Agatha. She smiled when Leesa Fredericks came in to feed the boys, holding Agatha's hand.

"No, no, NO! I want to play with Ainia." She tried to pull away, fighting the woman.

"All of you need to have your lunch," the long-suffering wet-nurse told the child.

"No, p'way," she lisped.

"Agatha," Abigail said in a stern voice, and the four-year old immediately ceased her whining, standing still when she saw her mother. "Can you handle them all?" she inquired of the woman who had been her twin's nursemaid and was now their nanny. The former wet-nurse's own child had come with them, so there was quite the houseful of young children.

"Ah, Brodie will be joining me, she will," the Scotswoman told the countess, giving her a curtsy.

"That's good," Abigail told her as she watched the woman expertly handling her daughter. She knew she didn't give her maid enough work with her clothes to take care of, and Brodie enjoyed the children.

Leesa was a far cry from the sour woman her husband had hired so long ago. In her care, the children were now happy and healthy, and Abigail was relieved they had made it out here safely. Yes, she'd chosen a poor time to go in search of Melissa Lawrence, but she was grateful for the home she had found here. She'd come to Australia for Melissa, who didn't want or need her. Now, she just needed to decide what to do with her own life. She could go back to England, but, with her father there and his already having tried to kidnap her children and get her money, she would have to live with continual guards for protection and constant worry. She was troubled less about herself than her children, who were growing so fast and strong, and she didn't want her father or his heir, her brother getting ahold of them. The men with her who were guards were already indiscernible from the stockmen who worked for Melissa, and they move freely about the station, not glued to her side at every turn. The question remained: what was she going to do with her life?

OUTBACK FUTURE

CHAPTER SEVEN

Abigail was surprised when Alinta took an interest in the embroidery that kept her fingers busy during the long, rainy evenings. As she sat in Mel's parlor, keeping herself busy when she wasn't reading, the station owner's wife joined her more often, as her pregnancy advanced and she became uncomfortable. The rainy season was in earnest, so she could no longer ride. Mel walked with her when she wasn't busy elsewhere on the station, but Alinta was pretty much confined to the house otherwise, which meant the two women spent more and more time together.

"Would you like to learn how to do this?" Abigail had asked, delighted to teach the woman.

Mel had been astonished to see her wife learning how to do the frivolous activity. Alinta was even more surprised when she learned Mel not only knew how to do the art but could make even fancier stitches than

the ones Abigail had been teaching her. With the silks catching on her dried and work-roughened hands, Mel showed Alinta and Abigail her own stitches. The needle didn't mind the state her hands were in, and the patterns were amazing. Her work was simply beautiful.

They'd spent a delightful evening after dinner in the warm parlor, the three of them embroidering squares of fabric that Abigail had determined to make into a throw for the couch as a thank you for letting her stay on the station. While Alinta wasn't very good yet, even her poor stitches could be hidden in the patterns until she learned and became better. Sometimes Mel would read to them as they stitched, stopping to explain something to Alinta when she didn't understand. The three women were companionable together, and sometimes the children joined them before they went to bed. Mel loved to read stories to the children, with Alinta listening as avidly as the little ones, who usually fell asleep before she was done.

"We should probably allow Agatha to join us at the table. How else is she going to learn her manners?" Mel had asked Abigail.

Alinta learned just as much by watching the other two. She became aware that not everything was English, not everything American. English was much more formal and American very casual. Mel hadn't quite been able to explain that to her before, but, by observance, she could see the differences between the two women. It wasn't just that Mel was a butch woman and Abigail very effeminate; it was how they were raised. She was determined that Ainia would be raised in this white world, and she caressed the babe she was carrying, hoping it, too, would be accepted into Mel's world.

"Me learn dress like English?" Alinta asked as they made themselves ready for bed.

"You want to learn how to dress like the English?"

At her eager nod, Mel nodded in return. "You dress any way you want to."

Mel watched her wife and unconsciously compared her to the many ewes they had growing bigger in the various paddocks. She checked regularly on those in the near vicinity, taking the time near the end of the rainy season to check on the flock and herd of horses in the new area they had claimed. They were doing fine, and she brought back several mares who hadn't bred with her herd stallion and let them go in with Diablo, hoping to get offspring from him. There were one or two she'd already left with him who were showing no signs of having taken, either, but she left them with him, hoping for good results. She knew he was still young, and she was looking forward to seeing his offspring in the coming years.

Abigail watched Alinta, too, seeing how solicitous Mel was with her and wishing she was the one pregnant, with Mel caressing the woman's stomach when she thought no one was looking. She tried not to be jealous, resigned to the fact that Mel loved this beautiful and simple woman. She realized that a lot of people would be prejudiced against these people who were of a different color, as two of her guards and Mrs. Fredericks had proven, and she had been shocked to find it out. She herself hadn't seen a black person until she moved to London. Alinta wasn't as dark as the tribe that lived across the creek, but she was darker than would be acceptable in, say Sydney, and certainly she would not be allowed in London except as a servant. She analyzed her own feelings on the situation, realizing they *were* people, just a different sort of people. She could see that Alinta had chosen to follow Mel's ways as evidenced by her interest in embroidery, books, and other things. None of the ones across the creek, even those who came to work for Mel, showed much interest in white man's ways,

but they liked to be able to buy the material to make clothing, boots, and some other white man's things. She had seen how Alinta valued the knife Mel had given her, a simple gift but of some meaning and value to the woman. She didn't know that Alinta's life had incomparably changed over the metal that was in this knife.

It was an interesting situation, and, as the rainy season drew to an end, Abigail began to get anxious about leaving. She found she didn't quite want to. While she knew she didn't want to stay in the outback forever, she would miss Mel, the only true friend she had on this Earth. She didn't count Gretchen, the friend she had made who knew Mel who was far away in London and hadn't answered her letter, not that she knew of. But then, none of Abigail's mail would have been forwarded here to the station and would be waiting for her in Sydney, if she returned there. That was the conundrum: would she return to Sydney? America sounded just as immense as Australia, and there were more people there. She wondered if her father was still looking for her. He would never find her here. Mel was her refuge; she was safe here. Her guards really had nothing to do here since she didn't need to be protected from anyone. She had encouraged them to learn what they could, to take on jobs to help out on the station and make themselves useful.

The end of the rainy season, while not turned off in one day, tapered off slowly. It also signaled a change in the pace around the station as hugely pregnant ewes lumbered around the paddocks. Many species of animals gave birth in the spring, and, while early in the season, they had several litters of dogs and one of cats. The children were delighted and fascinated

with all the animals and played in the garden that Abigail helped to lay out with the assistance of Mel and several employees in between the final rain showers. Alinta watched as they planted flowering plants and trees for shade, and one of the stockmen built some benches for sitting and enjoying the garden.

"I'll have to send to Sydney for flowers," Mel said with a smile as she and several men put down wood chips along the paths along with gravel.

"We have flowers," Alinta stated, smiling back at Mel. When she arched her back, her large stomach jutted out before her.

"There are some that don't grow here," she answered, eyeing her wife and wondering when exactly she was due. It could be anytime soon, and, between her and the ewes, it was going to be a busy time.

Alinta still had a hard time understanding the purpose of a garden like this, but then she had had to learn about a food garden. The stockmen's wives had delighted in teaching the woman its purpose. Now, with the English countess as her companion, the wives had held back, intimidated by the posh woman.

The cook, though, was elated to have a garden by the back doors, hiding the dunny out back and giving them raised beds for her to plant some herbs nearer to the house. Many times, kangaroos and other animals had eaten them from the gardens before they could be harvested. At least with the house there and more people about, they might frighten these animals away before they had a chance to eat the valuable spices she needed for their table.

It rained only occasionally now, the creeks were still quite full, as the land slowly drained, but things were drying out. Almost overnight, it seemed that a carpet of green was painted across the outback, turning desert-like conditions to fertile grass pastures. The sheep, horses, cows,

and other animals couldn't eat it fast enough, filling their gullets and putting on weight to be held against a time where there might not be any more of this rich and lush grass.

"I want to even out those fields over there and grow hay," Mel told her men, who had already started the work by removing waterlogged and downed trees as well as rocks from around the nearly flat fields she had in mind and rolling them to the sides into piles to be used later for various projects around the station. There was an unending supply of both stones and downed trees on this station.

Men came trudging up the tracks, having heard Lawrence Station was hiring for the coming season, and Mel and the head stockman, Peter, interviewed them, determined which paddock would be best for them, and sent them or took them there, explaining what was expected of them. Since it was a job for only a few weeks' worth of work, many of them were grateful for the unexpected find, as it would mean they could afford to buy boots, blankets, or other kit as they tracked along in the outback. Some might stay on if they were suited to the work, but most would move on to the next available job if they could find one. Many stations hired these men occasionally to help with the work on their remote stations. Lawrence was one of the first to call for men and actually offer a job in advance of the expected work.

CHAPTER EIGHT

The first ewes born in the home pastures signaled a wave of unending and exhausting work for the weeks to come. Mel was up and out early every morning. Alinta wanted to follow her, but her own exhaustion had her staying in bed longer and longer each day. She would look for Mel later in the day when she brought food to the men and women working in the home paddock helping the many ewes in labor. She herself could no longer bend over the ewes to help them; her stomach forbade that.

Unwilling to stick her hand inside a ewe, actually sickened at the idea, Abigail instead helped Alinta fetch food and water for the others, keeping fires burning around the large paddocks to help keep the food and people warm and to keep away the dingoes and other animals drawn by the scent of the many ewes giving birth. Abigail hadn't realized this aspect of wool production, and watching the many births was a surprise to her. And so

many of them gave birth without help that it seemed the flock grew by leaps and bounds daily. When it rained, it made everyone miserable. Abigail finally realized that rain or shine, these men or in the case of Mel and Alinta, women, continued to work endlessly to help the animals. The cold hadn't gone away either, and they all shivered in their long coats. When the wind blew with the remaining rains, it was miserable for man and beast.

Mel hadn't realized that when she offered to pay the wives of the various stockmen or the few swagmen who traveled with women, that she would be shocking the men. While some appreciated the additional wages, some didn't want to work with women. Mel had Peter keep the women who wanted to work in the home paddocks to alleviate some of the prejudices. She often wondered what those men who objected would say if they realized she, a woman, worked right alongside them for years.

It was about a week into the first wave of lambing that Alinta went into labor. She hid the first signs and slowly made her way back to the house with Abigail, their duties of bringing food and billies of tea to those working so hard with the ewes done for an hour or two. She watched the patrolling men, a few who would not or could not work with the sheep, mostly the countesses' guards, now walking around the far sides of the fires, watching for dingoes.

Alinta saw that the many children were playing in the garden together, chasing each other around. Four-year-old Agatha, with Joseph, Leesa's two-year old son, was there, as well as Ainia, who was also two. Abigail's one-year-old twins were there, too. At times, some of the stockmen's children were invited over, but the garden was special and for use of those who lived in the big house. Brodie, Leesa, and Bonnie had their hands full watching that large group.

As Alinta painfully made her way up the stairs into the house, she handed the basket she had been carrying off to the cook, thanking her for filling it and reminding her they would be going out in a couple of hours again. She paused briefly as she headed up the main stairs, watching how graceful Abigail looked and wondering if Mel would like to see her in such a dress as she wore then. The color was like nothing that Alinta had ever seen in nature, and it caught her eye. She couldn't remember seeing that vivid a blue even in the vast and every changing skies of the outback. She understood more about embroidery and the designs in the fabric. Lace was still something new to her and she'd been surprised that Mel knew how to make it and was willing to show her, someday.

The pain in her stomach told her she would have to hurry to get to her bed. She had told no one she was in labor. Mel was so busy working, the valuable sheep keeping all her attention, and she had barely made it back to the house to wash and sleep for a few hours each day before she was back working over the many sheep. Alinta tried to remember what they had done last time when she had given birth to Ainia, but it had only been her and Mel then. There were many women about her now, but they, too, were so busy with the house and with the children. She would do this alone.

Alinta washed herself, as Mel had taught her. Remembering when water had felt odd on her skin, she now enjoyed the cleanliness that Mel insisted upon. Hygiene had never been a concern when she was growing up, but even when she had her monthly flow, being able to wash away the gooey stickiness of the blood was a luxury she enjoyed. She left off her clothes, preferring to pull on her nightshirt to hide her body. Between contractions, she pulled out towels and rags, and when another burst of pain hit, she held onto the end of the bed and waited for the pain to pass.

Despite the fact that the rainy season was nearing its end, it was still cold, and she threw a couple of logs on the fire in their bedroom fireplace, almost crying out as a particularly hard contraction seized her. That one was much stronger than the ones previous. She barely made it to the bed, surprised at the strength of the contractions that seized her now. She began to panic, not remembering it hurting this much when she'd had Ainia, as her body broke out in a sweat. She tried to sit on the edge of the bed, throwing down the towels and rags she would need and gasping at the pain.

"Alinta, did you want to …?" Abigail asked, knocking on the door as she entered the room and saw Alinta in distress. "Are you in labor?" she asked, alarmed as she panicked. Her first thought was to get help, to call down the stairs to her people and tell them to go get Melissa. Just then they both heard a crack of thunder, accompanied by a downpour of rain. Mel was going to be busy enough, trying to save her sheep without worrying about her wife. She hurried to the gasping woman, closing the door behind her. The children would be brought up to the nurseries down the hall, the two rooms adjoining and allowing them to play indoors. They didn't need to see this, and Abigail didn't want to see this, either.

"What do you need me to do?" she asked, trying desperately to remember what she did when she had her twins. She had called for the doctor, of course, but she knew that wasn't an option here. What in the world was she going to do?

"Help … bed," Alinta gasped through the pains as she tried to get further on the bed, trying to spread the rags so as not to ruin the bed beneath her.

Abigail rushed to help her when she saw what she was trying to do, spreading the rags easily, but startled to see Alinta sweating in the room.

The fire was well-established, and she could see new wood had recently been put on the fire. "I should get someone to help … my servants …" she began, gesturing, but Alinta grasped her arm.

"Help … me … bed," she pidgeoned.

For the first time in a while Abigail realized that Alinta's grasp of English was not that good. She didn't mind, though; her snobbishness was long gone. She understood the woman perfectly, and she helped her to get on the bed further.

Alinta spread her legs as she lay back, waiting for the next contraction to hit and gasping when the pains struck again.

Abigail tried to think what she could do. Looking around, she realized there was no water. "I'll get you some water," she gasped, slipping out of Alinta's grasp to run to the adjoining bathroom. She hadn't noticed this before, but the bathroom here was much better than any she had seen, even in London. Many still used slop jars, but Mel had modern plumbing. She hadn't thought about it much, but, turning the tap, she had warm water on a washcloth in no time. She wrung it out and hurried back to apply it to Alinta's forehead, wiping down the sweat that was tricking down her dark face at her exertions.

Alinta was making no noise, but her head turned side to side as she fought the pain. She breathed hard—in through her nose and out through her mouth—panting as the pains came at her, time and again, and faster.

Abigail was beginning to feel alarmed as she watched the woman. Had she looked like this when she gave birth?

"Lady Worthington?" a voice called, along with a knock on the door. "Are you in there?"

"Brodie? Brodie! Come in here!" she demanded, wiping at Alinta's brow again. As the servant cautiously opened the door, her eyes widened

in surprise, seeing the sight of the station owner's wife in labor and her sophisticated English lady helping the Aboriginal woman. "Do you know anything about birthing a baby?"

The maid shook her head as she started to back out of the room.

"Don't you dare go anywhere. I need help here."

"Mayhap Bonnie or Leesa knows about helping a woman give birth," the maid replied. It had been different when the countess had given birth, the doctor had been there. She didn't know what she would have done if he hadn't been.

Abigail suddenly realized the passage of time. The children were probably taking their naps. "Go, quickly and ask them to come here. Someone can stay with the children, but come back with them!" she ordered.

The door had barely shut behind the maid when Alinta let out a horrible moan. She cut it off immediately, but the pain must have been horrendous as she started pushing against it. She instinctively knew to do this, but it felt even more painful as she spread her legs further. She fell back against the pillows, breathing hard as the contraction passed.

"It's okay Alinta, maybe Leesa or Bonnie will know what to do," Abigail tried to reassure her, dabbing at her brow again and then wiping the sweat from her cheeks and neck. "Should I go get Melli—" she started to ask and caught herself. "Mel?"

"No … Mel … plenty work," Alinta rasped out against the pain that was hitting her.

Just then the door was knocked upon again.

"Come in," Abigail answered for them both, relieved to see her children's nursemaid and wet-nurse. "Do either of you have any experience birthing babies?" At the shake of two very frightened heads

she was angry. "You've had a child Leesa; you don't know about birthing one?" Again, a shake of the head. "And how many babies have you been a nursemaid for, Bonnie? Don't you know anything about birthing one?"

"I gets them after they is born, ma'am," Bonnie excused herself. "But all we can do is try, can't we?" She began to roll up her dress sleeves.

Between the three of them, Abigail realized she would have to take charge, and she didn't remember much of the birth of the twins, born well over a year ago. So much had happened since then, she had put the pain of their births out of her mind. She did remember the doctor feeling between her legs. Oh, God, she was going to have to check and see how far along Alinta was. She didn't want to alarm the unpretentious woman. This couldn't be much harder than watching a foal being born, and she'd seen that a couple of times, even though no one knew that she had. They would have been shocked that a lady of her station had witnessed such an event.

"Okay, you two get things ready for the baby. There is hot water from the tap in there." She nodded towards the bathroom. "We've got plenty of rags here," she said, taking charge. "Alinta," she said, getting the attention of the woman who had begun to strain again, "I'm going to take a look and see if I can see the baby." She didn't ask; she was just warning her as she eased the gown up to look. She had never really looked when she made love to Mel, so she'd never seen what it looked like between a woman's legs. Suddenly, it struck her as odd that she was helping the love of her life's wife to birth their baby. She saw the wet flesh before her; it was rather revolting. Alinta was hairy there, and blood and liquid were coming from her, getting the hair matted. She realized that she was also seeing what looked like the head of a baby, or, at least, she hoped that was what she was seeing. Trying to swallow the lunch that wanted to come back up, she put on a smile and spoke through her teeth, "I see the head, Alinta.

Now push." She tried to sound cheerful, but she had barely managed to talk at all.

Alinta bore down, knowing she must expel the baby from her body. Her body was giving her the pains to help her, but it felt as though the baby was stuck. She strained, and she strained. They all waited. Too much time was going by, and she was weakening. They were all too inexperienced to realize this. It was becoming dangerous.

As Alinta rested between bouts of pushing, Abigail stopped to drink some water herself. The room was stifling hot from the fire, and heat came off the tiring woman in waves.

"Why isn't the baby out?" Leesa asked Bonnie in a whisper, but Abigail heard her.

"I think it's too big," she told the wet-nurse. "We need to push it out, and I don't know what to do."

"I've heard of pushing on the babe inside the womb," Bonnie told her in a frightened voice. "I ain't ever seen it, but I heard of it."

Abigail considered. Alinta was getting very pale. Maybe they should send for Mel. She might know what to do. But what if Mel didn't know or she didn't make it in time? It was then that Abigail realized, Alinta could die. Women died in childbirth all the time. It was why they had doctors. There were no doctors in this God-forsaken outback, that was for sure. They had to make due for themselves.

"You," she said to Leesa, "go down to the workers' houses and ask if any of the wives have ever midwifed or know how to deliver a baby. Run!" she ordered, pushing at the older woman. As Leesa left the room, she turned to Bonnie. "Go down to the cook and ask her, see what she knows and send someone to get Mel. We need her—um—" she shook her head as though to clear it, "him here!" Bonnie nodded and ran out of the

room, not noticing the gaffe. Abigail returned to Alinta, who was trying to push again. She looked between the legs again, but there was no progress; the babe did seem stuck. She thought some more about what Bonnie said about helping to push the baby, but she couldn't figure out how it could be done.

"I … get … up," Alinta gasped.

"You want to walk? You can't," Abigail easily pushed the laboring woman back against the pillows. The woman couldn't fight back; she hadn't the strength.

"No … walk … push," she got out before the pains took her away again. She was swimming in a wave of agony in between bouts of darkness.

Abigail didn't know what to do. If she waited for further help, something she should have sent for sooner, it might come too late. She worried her lower lip, biting at it in consternation, wondering what she should do.

Alinta tried to rise again, fight against the pains enveloping her body. She managed to get one leg off the bed, and Abigail reached to put it back up but then realized that perhaps standing would help get the babe out of its mother's body. She backed away and helped Alinta to get her other leg across the bed and over the edge.

Alinta gasped at the pain. It felt new and extra intense, but she didn't care as she sat on the edge of the bed. She scooted forward, intending to squat. She now understood something her mother had once told her about childbirth, that the Earth would come for the babe, that it would draw it from the mother's body and help to birth it. She instinctively pulled herself over the edge of the bed, leaning against the wool filled mattress,

her lower back hurting so bad she almost gasped aloud. She spread her legs in a wide squat.

"What are you doing?" Abigail asked, but saw Alinta was about to fall.

"Baby … come … now," Alinta panted through her heavy breathing, her nostrils were flaring as she gulped in the air. She bore down and finally felt movement.

As Abigail watched, she realized that Alinta was too high up. If the baby came now, it would hit the wood floor. Already droplets of fluid and blood were streaking down the woman's legs and pooling around her feet. Abigail quickly put down rags and had just reached for a towel when she heard a small, weak cry. She looked up at Alinta, surprised at her making such a noise, but the woman had her face scrunched tightly as she concentrated and pushed. It was then that she realized it must be the baby. It wasn't dead, and she wanted to see if she could help it. She raised Alinta's gown and was shocked to see a bloody baby, halfway between the squatting woman's knees and coming out fast. She grabbed hold of it with the towel, unknowingly turning it. She saw that the cord holding it to the woman was wrapped around its neck. She knew from the horses she had seen born and discussed that this had to be moved and quickly grasped it. Just then Alinta gave a mighty push and the baby fell into the towel she was holding. Abigail barely caught the babe as her hand came up from moving the cord. She lowered the child quickly to the floor, as Alinta fell back against the bed and started to slip down the side.

"Wait, wait," Abigail warned her, pushing her back up. She wasn't strong enough. Just then two women opened the door, stopped upon seeing the countess on the floor pushing up at the station owner's wife. "Grab her before she falls!" she ordered, gasping at Alinta's weight. "She

hasn't passed the placenta yet," she added. That was the next step, she remembered.

The two women, one of them Leesa, quickly pulled Alinta back upright. She had passed out, and, as she was stood upright, the placenta began to come out of her body, still attached to the weakly crying baby lying on the towel on the floor.

Abigail pulled the baby on the towel into her arms and grabbed another towel to start cleaning it. She looked up at Alinta whose eyes fluttered weakly to see the babe, before closing again. Her head fell back, totally unsupported by the two women holding her up by the arms.

"We have to get her back in bed, get the placenta out, and get this baby cleaned up," the one woman, one of the workers' wives stated. She gestured to Leesa, who helped her get Alinta partially back into the bed, staining the material of the mattress with fluids.

"Do you have any thread?" the woman asked, letting Alinta go.

Abigail, holding the crying baby shook her head. Then her eyes scanned the room, and she spotted the embroidery threads. "There," she said, nodding towards the basket.

The woman quickly went over to the basket, pulled a skein of thread out, and quickly cut two pieces. She returned to the bed and tied off the cord in two places, using the sharp scissors between them to separate the cord from the babe.

"We need to get the placenta out," the worker's wife repeated to the other women, and no one stopped her as she pushed on Alinta's stomach.

As Alinta awoke, she screamed, the first real sound she had made since her labor began. She tried to fight the woman off, but she was too weak. The pain was dreadful, and she passed out again, the blood gushing

between her legs that were still hanging over the edge of the bed. She went completely limp again, and her body began to slide off the bed.

"Come on!" the woman said to Leesa, trying to prop the woman up and push on her stomach at the same time. The placenta dropped out with a loud plop. Goo splattered everywhere over the wooden floor.

Abigail stared in horror at the mess.

"Let's pack this off and get her and the babe cleaned up," the woman said, trying to get Alinta back up on the bed. "If she loses too much blood she'll die."

Abigail quickly put the babe down on the floor in front of the dresser and away from the bed. It was still faintly crying, but it sounded a little stronger with each cry. She helped them get Alinta settled in the bed, the already soiled rags and towels taken out from under the woman and placed over the mess on the floor. They packed more rags between Alinta's legs, and Abigail hurried to get the washcloth wet again, as well as a few rags. They cleaned her as best they could and found another gown to put her in, washing her naked body. She didn't awaken, and this concerned the Englishwoman.

Expertly, the woman, who introduced herself as Clementine, washed and cleaned up the baby. He had finally begun to cry like a normal newborn once he was splashed with water. The woman was shocked to find that water came from the taps and didn't need to be pumped. Finding there was both hot and cold water was also a novelty to her, but she was busy cleaning the gunk from the crying baby. She took the fresh towels that Leesa offered her and swaddled the babe snugly.

"Do you think she will live?" Abigail asked as they put the babe next to Alinta's warmth. Alinta hadn't woken yet.

"I don't know," Clementine admitted. "Aborigine women ain't like us," she said, indicating the three of them who were white. "Some is stronger, some ain't so much."

Abigail almost said that could be said about any women, but she kept her mouth shut. She didn't know if she could have done what that woman had done in tying off the cord, much less pushing the placenta from Alinta's body. "Let's set about cleaning this mess up," she said instead, almost slipping on one of the wet rags.

"You'se might like to wash up yerself," Clementine pointed out, and, for the first time, Abigail became aware that her gown was ruined. She hadn't even noticed the blood and muck covering her hands, arms, and clothes; she'd been too concerned with trying to help her friend. And that's what Alinta was to her: a friend. She looked at the woman and realized what she felt for Mel had been different, but, once she had accepted that Mel could only ever be a friend, she had extended that friendship to her wife. She knew Mel could never be hers again. The young girl she had been, the Mel she had loved so desperately, was never going to be hers. Couldn't be hers. This woman held Mel's heart, and she urgently wanted her friend to not know the grief of losing either the mother or the child. She realized the babe, a large boy, was cuddled in close to its unconscious mother.

"Yes, you are right," she agreed as Clementine and Leesa began to make sure that the rags were all over the mess they had made, using towels when they ran out of the rags.

As Abigail left the room, Bonnie came running up, out of breath. "Mel … he's coming," she gasped.

"Where have you been?" Abigail asked, wishing that the maid had been there to help. She looked at the woman, her hair wet and plastered to her

head and her dress entirely soaked. She was dripping on the carpet and wood floor.

"I had to run down and tell him. The cook didn't know anything about birthing, and no one was about to send for the master," she panted out. She was taking in great gulping breaths. "Is it … is it … born?" she asked.

"Yes, it's a boy," Abigail said as she heard the front door open and Mel's voice booming through the house.

"Alinta! Alinta! I'm coming!" she shouted as she took the stairs two at a time, her rubbers still shedding rain as she ran. She stopped still as she saw Abigail and the state her dress was in. Her face showed her shock at the sight.

"You have a son," Abigail said with a smile, feeling happy for her friend.

"What happened to you?" Mel asked, concerned. Then, realizing what was on the ruined dress, asked in the same breath, "Alinta?"

"She's asleep," Abigail said diplomatically. "I didn't have time to change."

Mel brushed by her now that she had her answers. The raindrops on her slicker fell onto the carpet runners, but she didn't care as she opened her bedroom door to go in.

Abigail had seen the look of worry and concern, as well as pride, on Mel's face in that brief moment. She turned to go to her rooms. "Please check on the children and send Brodie to me?" she asked Bonnie who had finally gotten her breath back. "Then look after yourself and change your clothes. That cold will be the death of you!" she chastised slightly, but looked and sounded concerned.

"Aye, my lady," the servant responded, following her down the hall until Abigail went into her rooms.

Abigail tried to get out of her dress herself but the clasps were out of reach. The sight of herself in the mirror was horrifying, and she couldn't ever remember looking this … messy. She wondered for a moment how she had looked giving birth to Agatha, as well as the boys. Brodie came in and helped her out of the dress, clucking at how it was ruined by the fluids—blood and sweat—on the fine material.

"It was for a good cause," Abigail consoled her maid, proud to have helped Alinta but wishing she had been of more help, that she had known what to do. She worried about the unconscious woman and fervently hoped she truly was just exhausted from the birth.

"I'll draw you a bath, ma'am," Brodie told her.

As the countess soaked in the guest tub without any assistance, a novel idea when servants usually had to pump, heat, and carry buckets of water for the chore, she thought over all the strange and wonderful events and realizations of the last few hours.

OUTBACK FUTURE

CHAPTER NINE

Mel was elbow deep in a ewe when Bonnie came running through the rain to find her. The chit didn't have proper rain gear on and was soaked through her dress, her hair plastered to her head. "Mr. Lawrence! Mr. Lawrence!" she gasped, holding a stitch in her side because she had run all the way from the house. "Mrs. Lawrence is in labor," she got out before turning aside and throwing up her lunch.

"What?" Mel said as she finally caught the elusive lamb's leg she had been trying to grasp in the ewe's uterus. She straightened that out, and the ewe, sensing that she could push now, gave a mighty heave. By the time Mel stopped wincing from the tightening of the bands of flesh on her hand, the lamb was following her hand out of the passage. Mel hastily stood up. "You, come over here and see to this ewe for me," she called to one of the men who had just finished up with a ewe of his own. "My missus is

lambing," she joked as she hastily washed up in a bucket she had there for that purpose, and then she followed Bonnie who had ran back to the house as soon as she was sure Mel had heard the news.

Mel was only a couple of minutes behind the servant, continuing to wash her hands in the rain that was running off her raingear. She brushed them time and again against the rubbers, getting the last of the muck and gunk of the sheep off them before plunging them in a rain barrel at the corner of the house to thoroughly clean them one last time and going into the house. She called out to Alinta and ran up the stairs, nearly slipping on them with her long rain gear, the water dripping all over the floor not bothering her in the least. Calling for her wife again, she stopped short of her room when she saw Abigail with muck and blood all down the front of her fine London-made dresses. Speaking briefly with her, she continued into her bedroom, pulling off her hat and slicker and dropping them by the bathroom door. She went to sit on the edge of the bed and stared horrified at the mess covering the mattress. She could see more blood and fluids all over the material. The sheets and the mattress were all ruined. Her feet avoided the pile of rags, towels, and muck on the floor.

"What happened?" she whispered, staring in disbelief at Alinta, who looked pale to the point of gray, and instantly worried her wife was dying. Her eyes were drawn to a tightly wrapped package on the bed next to Alinta.

"Mel?" The voice that came from her ashen face sounded nothing like Alinta.

Mel worried that she was dying. Women died in childbirth all the time.

"We have son? Good baby?"

"He's here, Alinta, right next to you. Can't you feel him?" Mel asked, even more concerned. She watched him, his lips moving as though he were trying to suck. She picked him up to show Alinta.

"Fine baby," Alinta rasped, closing her eyes almost immediately.

Mel panicked, looking around at the Bonnie and Brodie. "You there, get some beef broth for the lady. You, take all these rags and get me some clean ones." She watched as the two women scattered, noting the placenta with the trailing end tied off with embroidery silks on the rags on the floor. She studied Alinta's face again and couldn't figure out what to do. She could see they'd put another gown on her, but she was still bleeding. Vital blood was leaving her and was slowly draining her strength. She glanced down on the son who had caused all this and back to the mother. Standing up with the son, she pulled out a dresser drawer and put the babe in it carefully, pushing the clothes aside to keep him safe.

Next, she went back to Alinta, careful to step over the muck and rags that was still on the floor, too much for the one woman to carry. She lifted the skirt of Alinta's gown and saw that she was still bleeding. In the bathroom, she grabbed the last of the towels and brought them back to the bed to tuck underneath her wife. When she lifted her slightly, she saw a tear that was bleeding rich, red blood. Remembering the embroidery silk, she quickly stepped to the basket and pulled a long white thread that already had a needle attached. She cut the end from the sampler that Alinta had been working on. She used this to poke at Alinta's flesh. The woman never even flinched. Taking a deep breath, Mel began to sew the flesh around Alinta's vagina together, being careful to match it up as evenly as she could. She could tell it had ripped, as the tear was ragged. Blood still oozed out between the threads, but it lessened as she sewed small, tight little stitches that held the gap closed.

"What are you doing?" Brodie asked, horrified as she caught sight of the work Mel was doing.

"I'm stitching her up. And you could help me if you found some more towels or rags and washed away the blood," she told her through clenched teeth, trying not to dig too deep or make the stitches uneven.

Shocked, Brodie tried to obey, but she found no more clean towels since they had used them all for the birth. She glanced at the babe in the dresser drawer, where the shirts were pushed aside, and reached for one to take it to the bathroom and use for cleanup. She ripped the shirt, wetted it, and wrung out the material under the warm water, leaving a bit so she could wash the missus.

"I have this," she said, holding out the saturated cloth and the dry half.

"My hands are full at the moment," Mel got out, gritting her teeth, almost done sewing the tear, despite the bloody mess. "Can you wipe it there?" She nodded towards where she was holding the last of the tear together with her fingertips. "I can't see."

Brodie's nose wrinkled as she did as she was asked, blotting at the skin. She was horrified with how much blood came away. The extra water dripped down to Alinta's anus and combined with the blood there, pooling on the towel before quickly absorbing into the material.

"More," Mel commanded, sewing quickly to finish. She could see the woman wasn't giving it her all, and she was desperate to finish. Alinta's color still was not good, and her breathing was coming in short, periodic gasps.

Brodie squeezed a little more of the water out as she reached, and Mel indicated that she should blot along the sutures and down along the crack towards the towel. Brodie likened it to the babes that she had changed

their diapers. She had never seen a woman's privates before and was shocked by it. Still, she bravely did as she was commanded.

Mel took pity on the woman once she had tied off the last of her stitches. The bleeding had stopped, and she took the ripped shirt, blotted until all the blood was gone, and used the dried portion to finish the cleanup. "Can you find her another gown? If not a gown, then one of my shirts," she advised. She briefly remembered one of the first times Alinta had worn one of her shirts, they had been huge on her.

Once they had changed Alinta's clothing, Mel lifted her up from the bed. "Have someone get some new sheets and change this bed," she ordered Bonnie, who had just walked in. She lifted Alinta higher and took her with her to sit in the rocking chair, cradling her wife in her arms as she looked down. She prayed silently as she gazed into the gray face of her beloved wife.

Mel watched the two women distastefully pull off the sheets from the ruined mattress. There were towels and rags within the dirty sheets, and they wrapped them to throw them on top of the last of the gunk on the floor. Brodie used a remnant of her destroyed shirt to wipe the floorboards of the blood that had begun to dry.

Two of Mel's maids came in then to change the sheets. Before long, Alinta was tucked in the bed, warm and dry for the first time in hours. Mel sat there, waiting for her wife to awaken. She'd changed out of her own wet clothes, her rubbers now hung up in their bathroom.

Mel sipped at the broth Bonnie had brought, hoping her wife would awaken and drink the rest. The babe was quiet lying next to its mother's warmth, perhaps it sensed that Alinta needed her sleep, perhaps it too was exhausted from its birth.

"Mel?" Alinta rasped finally, waking and moving her hands about restlessly.

"Hello, there," Mel whispered, leaning in, putting the broth on the side table. "Are you hungry?"

"So weak, so weak," she said, her hand encountering the baby's warmth and stilling as she rested her hand on it. "Babe okay?"

"The baby is fine. You delivered a healthy baby boy," she said, wondering if Alinta remembered their earlier conversation.

"So weak," she rasped again.

Panicking a little, Mel said, "I have broth here. I want you to eat it. It will help you get your strength back. You need to get your strength," she admonished, almost as though Alinta had to be chastised.

"So weak," she repeated.

"I need you strong for the baby. Now, sip this," she said as she held the spoon to her wife's mouth. Slowly, spoonful by spoonful she fed Alinta, who soon enough tired but managed to get some of the broth inside. Mel finished the rest, but by then it was cold.

The babe started to cry and Alinta didn't move. Mel knew it was seeking nourishment and wondered how long they could go without feeding the boy. She didn't remember what they had done for Ainia, Alinta had effortlessly handled all of that herself. She didn't know if anyone on the station was breast feeding; she hadn't paid attention.

"Sir?" One of the maids was at the door. "Is there anything I can get you?"

"I'll want some more broth for the missus, and I'd like some stew for myself," she ordered. "Maybe some of those biscuits to sop up my gravy?" She was ravenously hungry. Then she thought to ask, "Are there any nursing mothers on the station?"

"Nursing mothers?" the maid asked, confused.

Mel turned and got up, handing the now empty bowl to the woman. "Yes, our baby may need to be nursed. The missus isn't up to the task at the moment."

"I could check in the village sir, but I don't know …"

"Are you saying none of the *white* women would nurse my son?" Mel asked, sounding suddenly angry.

"No, sir, I ain't saying that," the woman said, but her blush betrayed her thoughts.

"Get out of here," Mel snarled, now definitely angry. She turned to Alinta and their son. Alinta still looked gray, but she didn't know if she had a tad more color or she was just imagining it. The broth would help strengthen her, but would Alinta be able to pull through? Who knew how much blood she had lost? She saw the babe squirming in its sleep and turned back to the door to open and go through it, shutting it gently behind her so as not to awaken her wife or baby.

"How is she?" Abigail asked, coming up in a new gown, looking all fresh and clean.

"She bled a lot," Mel said, calming her anger. "I may need to find a nursemaid." She went to go downstairs.

"I have a nursemaid for my boys. Why don't we ask her?"

"She wouldn't mind?"

"Leesa? Now, why would she mind? I pay her for both of the boys, when I could have only paid her for one. I'm more than fair with her and her wages."

"No, I meant she wouldn't mind feeding an Aborigine baby?"

Abigail looked on in surprise, her mouth forming a perfect O. "I never thought to ask, but maybe we should?" She turned to walk back to her

rooms, the nursery between the master bedroom and the guest bedrooms. They could hear the children playing in the far room. Abigail stuck her head in, but the children didn't see her. She waved at Mrs. Fredericks, gesturing her to the door. When the woman had walked across the room, Abigail asked, "Leesa, would you help Mrs. Lawrence? The babe will need feeding."

Mel saw the expression on the woman's face and turned away before she replied. She already knew the answer and wasn't willing to listen to the prejudice she saw there. Abigail didn't realize Mel was gone when Leesa answered.

"Um, no miss, I wouldn't care to," she admitted.

"It's just a babe, a newborn. He won't drink much, but he will need …" she began, arguing the babe's case and glancing back at Mel for help, but Mel was walking down the steps already. She turned back to her nursemaid. "You would seriously let a babe starve?"

"I's signed on to help you'rn babies. Not black babies."

"It's not a black baby, it's …" she began but realized her words were futile. It wasn't her place to say who this woman fed, short of her own children. Rising up slightly, remembering who she was and this was an employee, she pointed out, "I let you keep your son Joseph with us when other employers would have turned you out. I suggest you think about that as you wean my sons off your ample bosom, when you could have helped my friend." She turned and followed after Mel.

Leesa Fredericks had gotten used to the Lady Worthington's easy-going ways. She'd been a delightful employer and almost a friend to her and her son, as they made their way during that extended voyage on the ship and the relentlessly long trip across Australia to this oasis.

Mel had to return upstairs to find her rubbers so she could go out in the torrential rain to look for a wet-nurse. She was gone a long time. She'd checked with her stockmen and none of them had a woman who was feeding little ones—or so they said. She was certain if she had asked the wives, one or two of them would have helped Alinta, but it was too late for that, now. She found a woman wading across the bridge to the village, the water rising to dangerous levels. There was some confusion about her borrowing the woman versus buying her, but Mel sorted it out—she hoped—and the woman had fetched a few things and brought her own babe, following behind Mel as best she could. The woman spoke little English, and her name, which she'd had to repeat several times, sounded like Kug. Mel didn't know if the rain washed the woman thoroughly before she got back to the big house, but she hadn't wanted to explain about cleaning herself. She led her inside, and the maids already had seen them coming, had towels waiting for them to dry off. She helped the woman, holding the babe as she dried off and looked about wonderingly at the strange house with fear and awe. Mel handed the baby back to her and hung up her own rubbers

Leading Kug upstairs, Mel was surprised to see Mrs. Fredericks already there, rocking the babe as she fed her. Gesturing to the babe, she couldn't make herself understood to the Aboriginal woman, who crouched down on her haunches in a corner and waited. The room was warm with the fireplace, and the woman seemed to enjoy the feel of it.

"You can also feed the babe through the night from your wife's teats," Mrs. Fredericks whispered to Mel.

"Changed your mind?" Mel asked sardonically, an eyebrow raised.

Blushing the woman shook her head. "I'm sorry. That was silly of me. Your missus has been so kind to me and the children. It would be poor repayment if I didn't help her in her hour of need."

Mel nodded in agreement, not sure what else to say. Her anger had dissipated somewhat, but not completely. The long walk through the rain, the constant inquiries at the various cottages, and the walk over the bridge to the village had cooled much of her anger. Still, she wasn't used to this type of prejudice. She knew her own people had them but dared not speak them in her presence. Now, she realized there was a lot more going on than she had seen before. She had probably ignored it in the past or just simply been unaware of it. She shook her head at her own foibles, unaware of the prejudices that had been brought to her attention this day.

CHAPTER TEN

It was touch and go for many days as Alinta slowly recovered. Mel slept beside her at night and did hold the baby to Alinta's breasts, helping the babe eat. It was awkward and trying, but, still, she managed. She knew those first meals were important for the babe, something about the first mother's milk. During most of the day, Leesa and Kug were feeding the baby, taking turns. Kug liked the white man's room, sleeping in the corner to help with the missus.

"How is she doing?" Abigail whispered, checking on them once again on the third day. Mel hadn't left Alinta's side, and Abigail wondered if her friend would have been that diligent to her but quashed the thought before it caused pain. It wouldn't do to speculate like that, but one question continued to nag at her thoughts. Mel was faithful to her wife, but how had Alinta become pregnant, and twice at that?

"I simply don't know. I managed to get more broth in her. I carried her to the toilet, and she cried when her stream hit the stitches," she confided soto-voiced. "She's sleeping now. I washed the sweat from her, and just that seemed to have worn her out."

"Mel, you need to get out, too. The baby is being fed." She nodded towards the rocking chair which Kug found fascinating as she sat in it with the babe. "You need to eat and get out for a while. This is a sick room, and it's beginning to smell like one." She had noticed it when she first walked in.

Mel nodded, agreeing. "I should check on the sheep ..." she murmured, but looked back at Alinta with worry.

"I'll watch her. I've arranged for a new mattress to be made, and I've been sewing the edges," Abigail confided.

"New mattress?" Mel asked, glancing at the English woman in surprise.

"The old one got rather mucked up. The sheets are hiding it now, but I'm certain you could use a new one. Your servants said you stuff it with wool?"

Mel nodded, having forgotten that part of things and then sighed. Her brain felt fogged in from everything that had happened since the birth. "Do you think Alinta looks better?" she asked hopefully, needing some sign that her wife was going to survive the traumatic birth.

"I can't tell in this light. When it is sunny again, we should open these windows and air out the room," Abigail said brightly. She remembered how the room had stunk after her husband's death and worried that this room was becoming just as smothering.

"Aye, we should," she agreed and then shut the door as she left the room, glancing at her wife one more time. She pushed aside thoughts of

Alinta nearly dying, that she could still die, and what she, Mel, would do if Alinta did.

"Papa!" Ainia called as Mel walked into the nursery, not having seen his daughter in days. She caught the child up and swung her, pleased to see the young girl looking hale and hearty. "Mama better?" she asked, worried.

"She's getting there. She gave birth to a fine brother for you."

"Don't want bother. Want Mama," she said stoutly and Mel laughed at the word she got wrong.

"Well, my darling, little girl. You will have to wait until Mama is feeling better. Until then, are you being a good girl for me?"

The two-year-old nodded solemnly. "Down, down," she cried, seeing one of her new friends playing with a toy she liked and running off when Mel put her down to play with the others. Mel smiled indulgently.

"They are going to miss her when we go," Abigail said as she watched her children play with Mel's.

"Are you leaving soon?" Mel asked, looking up.

"I think after the wool is gathered, so we can ride with them," she responded. "Won't that be safer?"

Mel nodded thoughtfully. "I think you should meet Carmen Pearson before you head east to Sydney."

"That's your friend who raises the horses, right?"

"Yep, she would love to talk to you about horses. I want to arrange to buy a couple of your Thoroughbreds too. I think breeding them with the Brumbies and Carmen's horses out here will provide us with horses that will have universal appeal. I'd like to see what we get from the offspring."

"Well, sounds like you already have this thought out. I never said I'd sell my Thoroughbreds," she teased as they left the nursery.

"Yours aren't the only ones in England. Hell, if I remember correctly, my father got some really good ones from the continent."

They bantered back and forth as they went downstairs, dressed in their rubbers, and headed out, still chattering about horses.

Mel was pleased that the men had carried on without her. She knew they would, but the results were astonishing to see. Already most of the home paddock sheep had given birth, and the men, if they weren't helping a sheep to give birth, were docking and mulesing the lambs. Mel hated this part of raising sheep, but it was better to have it done before flies became a bother and infected the wounds. Mel freely gave compliments on the men's work, clapping a few on the back and thanking them. This was something most station-owners didn't do, and the men were always surprised, but they appreciated Lawrence for his fairness and his recognition of their work. They expressed their concern over the missus, acknowledging that word had filtered down from the big house that the birth had been especially difficult for the petite woman. No one mentioned about their missus' being unavailable to help feed the baby, but Mel remembered who they were and decided to get rid of them. She send them out into her far paddocks to work, along with their families, and they could quit if they didn't like it. She wouldn't tell them directly that their prejudice could have killed her baby, but she felt that and she might eventually let it slip to someone who would surely talk.

In the meantime, she was pleasant to all and talked sheep until Abigail wandered off, drawn back to the stables where only riding horses were and beyond it to take treats down to the valley where Diablo waited for Alinta but settled, distrustfully, for the English woman.

"He's going to be something when he's full grown," Mel said, coming up behind her after she'd watched Abigail try to build rapport with the

young stallion with no success. He'd put up with her pats while she gave him treats, but, when she tried to sweet talk him and pet him more without treats, he shied away and went back to his mares.

"He sure has a mind of his own. He loves Alinta," she said wryly, laughing at herself as he trotted away, his tail up and cocked, his neck rising to look over his small harem. On alert, he checked that they were where he wanted them and that there were no threats to them around.

"I can understand that," Mel replied. She looked up the trail into the valley and then back towards the house. She could see her bedroom windows and immediately thought about returning. She hadn't been gone too long, but long enough, and she wanted to see how Alinta was faring. Beyond the house, storm clouds were whipping by. Only one or two promised rain, and there was no way to tell if they would hit this area or go around.

"I'm sorry, Mel, I didn't understand before. I do now," Abigail said, putting her hand on her friend's arm, squeezing it, and dropping it just as quickly.

"Understand what?" Mel asked. She walked with Abigail up the trail and adroitly avoided a fresh horse plop.

"That you love Alinta. I really thought once I got here that you would fall into my arms, relieved that I had come so far for you."

"You did, eh?" Mel asked, amused. "What you and I had was in our youth. I still love you," she said, and Abigail's heart leapt at the admission, "but as a friend now. I hope never to lose that friendship."

Abigail wanted to clutch at her chest; her heart was beating so hard she could hear the pulse in her ears. She smiled wryly. "You have my friendship," she admitted softly. "Always."

"Good. You were right, I needed to get out and take a walk. I feel refreshed. Now, I need to get Alinta stronger and our son under her care."

Abigail felt as though with that statement that Mel willed it to happen. Day by day Mel fed Alinta broth, carried her to the bathroom, cleaned her, and held their son to her breast. When Alinta was awake that first day after their walk, she took her downstairs and out to the porch while the maids changed the bed, taking the soiled mattress out and exchanging it for another, stuffed full of fresh, clean wool. The windows were opened wide as the maids hurriedly aired and cleaned the room, rubbing the wood with wax polish and making it smell clean and fresh. The bathroom, too, was scrubbed. Before Mel returned Alinta to the bed, she washed her gently and changed her gown before tucking her into the fresh sheets. She then took the boy baby from Kug, who had nursed him to satiation, and tucked him in beside his mother. From that day on, Mel carried Alinta outside daily so she could watch the station from the front porch. Mel made sure she was well covered, gently wrapping the blankets around her herself. Women from the station and the village came by to pay their respects almost every day; it was how Mel learned which had been breast feeding and who was married to which of her men. When she spoke to Peter Winston and gave him a list of men she wanted moved into certain paddocks, he was surprised but didn't question the station owner's requests.

"We'll send them out with the sheep after the stockman brings them in for shearing," she told him. "If they don't want the job, then pay them off and they can be on their way with the shearers."

"What about the stockmen whose sheep will be brought in?" he asked.

"See where they might want to go with another flock," she replied, dismissing the subject.

He had his orders, and those on that list were going to be gone. No longer would they have the amenities afforded them at the home station. Not all stations allowed stockmen to bring their wives and family, but despite her generosity, not one of them had stepped up and helped her when she needed them for Alinta and her as yet unnamed son.

"What shall we name him?" Mel asked Alinta.

Today, finally, she was looking healthy. Her cheeks were slightly flushed from the wind that blew across the porch, where both she and the baby were wrapped in quilts and warm as they enjoyed the fresh air.

"What was your papa's name?" Alinta asked.

"Victor," she told her wife with a little grin.

"Veetor?" Alinta tried to wrap her tongue around the name and, unable to do so, frowned.

"What was your father's name?" Mel asked, grinning at her attempt to say the name.

Alinta frowned deeper. She tried not to think of her people, especially her father, who would have rejected her if she had come back to him. To him, she was damaged goods; her value completely gone after being taken. Still, she wondered if her mother had been accepted back, her father forgiving her for the white men who had captured her. She looked away as she answered Mel, "Omeo."

"Hmmm, I don't think that name would fit out here, either."

"Fit?"

"Well, a good, strong baby like that should be named after a good, strong man." Mel thought of all the men she had admired over the years. There were only a few of them, and none of their names seemed fitting. She glanced up as she heard a clattering of hooves on rock and saw that Diablo had come up the path and was looking for feed or treats at the barn. "Maybe we should name him Diablo," she teased, indicating the young stallion who was posturing for his mares, who had followed him up from the valley.

Alinta laughed, knowing Mel was teasing her, but her eyes glistened upon seeing the young stallion. She had missed him while she recovered from the birth of her son. She understood what Mel was saying: their son should have a solid name.

Abigail joined them and suggested a few names that were decidedly English. Mel wrinkled her nose at Abigail when she mentioned one name in particular. Alinta liked the name Robert, but that was Abigail's brother's name and both Abigail and Mel said no on that one but didn't explain why.

They went through quite a few names, and Alinta stopped contributing, as she didn't know too many white man's names except for those men she had met on the stations. She became more passive and just spoke up when a name came close to her own people's words. "What about a Greek god's name like you give Ainia?" she finally asked. She was still a little confused as Mel had even *asked* her. In her tribe, the father just made this decision. These English were very odd sometimes. Then, understanding a little more, she corrected herself mentally: this American was odd. Mel was completely different than the others she knew here on the station, whatever their nationality.

Abigail and Mel had a lot of fun with working through the Greek names, from Apollo to Zeus, but Alinta didn't understand them and they didn't always explain why it was so funny. Mel could see her wife was becoming annoyed and began to get serious. She knew it wasn't fair to talk above her, when Alinta hadn't had the opportunity to read the books that they had.

Finally, Mel said, "How about Mackenzie? Mackenzie Lawrence," she said, letting the name roll off her tongue.

"Who was that?" Abigail asked, wondering if she had heard the name before. They had, after all, gone through quite a list of people they had known, even combining a few for first and middle names.

"No one that I know. How about you?" Mel asked, looking at Alinta who was starting to get sleepy-eyed. She worried that she had kept her wife outside too long that day. With the sun was shining for a change, she'd lost track of the time.

Surprised at being asked, Alinta woke from her sleep stupor. "No name I know," she pidgeoned.

Mel grinned; she had figured as much. "I kind of like it. It sounds strong, and we can shorten it to Mack."

"Mack Lawrence," Abigail murmured, liking it as well. "But what about his middle name?"

"We'll put Victor down?" Mel asked her wife, who nodded sleepily. Mel smiled and leaned down, took the baby and handed him to Abigail, before picking her wife up in her arms.

"Veetor?" Alinta murmured sleepily, snuggling into Mel's arms and laying her head on her husband's shoulder

Mel laughed quietly as she waited for Abigail to open the screen door so she could carry her wife back upstairs. Every day she was getting

stronger, and Mel couldn't be more relieved. She deposited her wife in their bed and tucked her in. Abigail handed the baby to Mel. She put Mack down in the bassinet they had beside the bed and smiled, Mackenzie Victor Lawrence. Her father might not have approved her choice of mates, but he would definitely approve of her strong and healthy son. Glancing up as Ainia ran into the room, she grabbed her daughter before she could wake Alinta.

"No, no, NOOOO! Mama!" the child whined and squirmed to get out of her father's arms, as Mel hushed her and closed the door softly behind them.

"Ainia, Mama needs to sleep. Are you dressed to go outside because I want to show you something?" Mel asked to distract her.

"Ready!" the two-year-old squealed, suddenly intrigued and easily distracted.

Mel shushed her daughter and then scrutinized the outfit, convinced it was not something the child should wear outside.

"Me, too!" another voice piped up, and Mel looked past her daughter to see Agatha gazing at her hopefully.

"Are you dressed to go outside, Lady Worthington?" Mel asked the girl.

"Yes," she lisped shyly, not used to being addressed so formally.

"Well, if you two would like to see something, I found a nest that had babies in it."

Both girls were instantly intrigued and ready. Mel carried Ainia down the stairs, and Abigail followed along, hand in hand with Agatha, grinning at her friend who had kept the girls from waking Alinta. She was taking fewer naps, but any sleep was good for the recovering mother.

Mel led them around the play yard, where a couple of trees stood and pointed to the nest. "Now watch, and, if you are really lucky, the babies might peek out."

The four of them watched the nest avidly, and, just when the girls were losing interest, an adult bird flew in, staring suspiciously at the humans. Then they all heard the peeps of baby birds from inside the nest.

"There," Ainia said, pointing, but the vision of a fuzzy head was only fleeting. The sides of the nest were high enough to hide the babies in it. Mel had seen the nest from her bedroom window and knew there were three eggs in it, and she'd seen that they had all hatched.

"What kind are they?" Abigail asked softly, having picked up Agatha so she could see better.

"Magpies," Mel answered just as softly.

"How many are there?"

"I think three, but it was hard to see, and, as you can see now, mom— or is that dad? —doesn't like our presence here." The bird was still eyeing them, turning its head and looking fiercely at each of them. "Well, I don't think we are going to see much, but you two can go play. I see Leesa and Bonnie have come out with Joseph, and I'm sure you will want to play with him." She put down Ainia, who ran off at Mel's suggestion.

Abigail had barely put Agatha down, when she ran off even faster than her friend. She smiled, knowing her daughter was enjoying herself more than she would have back at Hedgerows, the ancestral estate for the Worthington family. She still shuddered at the thought of that horrible woman who had run the house for her husband.

"Look!" Mel took a breath, pointing at the clothesline behind the house. An adult magpie was on the line, upside down, and worrying a frayed end of the line.

"Pretty birds," Abigail responded, whispering. She has never taken note these birds while walking through the garden. They weren't as bright or as colorful as the parrots and cockatoos that flew over in large flocks.

"They are. They must feel really comfortable with the house here to build their nest there," she pointed at the one above them, and they started to walk back to the house.

"Mr. Lawrence, sir?" One of the employees approached.

"Yes, Jacob. What can I do for you?" Mel answered, inwardly laughing as she thought about how odd it really was to be called mister.

"Peter asked that I fetch you. He's in the shearing shed."

"I'll be right there," she responded.

"I want to see," Abigail said as Mel turned around to make her goodbye.

"Okay." Mel started walking towards the barns and sheds, looking for her head stockman. She found him in the main shearing shed, the largest one, where there were tables already set up to sort the fleeces, prior to the start of shearing. The rains were nearly at an end, and, with the sun coming out more and more, it was time. The many flocks in the outlying paddocks would be coming in soon, to be there when the shearers arrived. Wagons would soon be bringing the stations supplies for the year and then load up and take their huge bales of fleece, and Mel wanted the station to be ready for them.

"Hey, Lawrence," the man greeted Mel, leaving off the mister. "We need to knock out more of these for sorting ..." He indicated some tables he had been mending, and so, the discussion regarding how they'd sort the sheep, the wool, and grade it began. It went on for a good hour as they talked and organized, setting up for the coming work.

Abigail watched, impressed with the size of the buildings and her friend's knowledge and command of his employees. She didn't realize the half of it.

OUTBACK FUTURE

CHAPTER ELEVEN

The next week, Mel found a baby magpie had fallen out of the nest and brought it into the house to keep it safe from the barn cats. She fed it scraps from the kitchen and made a little cage to keep it from the housecats and anyone else who got too curious. When she fed it four times a day, it squawked every time it saw her enter the room, its call attracting wild magpies at the windows. They watched Mel through the panes as she took time before and after her breakfast for the baby bird that was growing fast, again after lunch, and then before dinner. Always, there were magpies watching through the window as she interacted with this young bird. When she was busy working, Alinta or one of the servants was set to feed the small bird as much as it wanted, at almost any time of day, and still the wild magpies watched.

The cries of the small magpie also attracted the children, eager to feed it themselves. Gently, Mel and Alinta allowed the children to feed it. The children were also being judged by the wild magpies as they looked through the windows at the strange humans feeding one of their own.

Sheep shearing began as the mulesing and docking were done, the lambs that survived having healed from the horrible ordeal. Large wagons full of men who did the shearing arrived at the home station. The bunkhouses were packed full. The men were foul-mouthed and dirty, but Lawrence Station provided baths and showers for them. A few even used them, taking the time to wash out their sweaty and dirty clothes, if they owned extra.

Abigail watched in amazement as Mel coordinated her men, bringing 'round vast flocks of sheep and getting them to and through the shearing setups, where the shearers worked through them skillfully and quite quickly. Abigail's back ached just watching them. They flirted outrageously with her, but she had learned to turn a deaf ear to their course language and leers. Mel admonished a couple of them who went over the line, but, for the most part, she told Abigail to stay away if she didn't want to hear it. Abigail saw that Mel's size and the rumors of her fists kept several of the men in line. She even witnessed Mel bunching up the shirt of one man, preparing to strike him, when the apology that issued forth from the frightened man's lips stopped her friend from hitting the man. It showed a new side of Mel that Abigail admired. Once again, she wished the large woman could have been hers, realizing what she had lost through the years. She envied Alinta for the love she saw Mel heap on her,

knowing it could have been hers had she been brave enough to take it back in the day. She knew, though, that she couldn't have lived like this, openly with her partner who everyone thought was a man.

The number of bales began to pile up in the barns, every available space taken up by these large sacks of wool. Abigail had thought it would all be dirty and unclean, but Mel's men sorted it, sometimes by breed, as different sheep had different kinds of wool and Mel didn't want to get docked and lose money for the combination. The tables came in handy to sort and hold loose fleeces so the men could shove the wool into large bags that made up the bales, some standing in the bale and packing it down to get the most out of it.

More and more sheep were herded down the tracks from the far paddocks, the men knowing it was time for the yearly shearing. The next day the stockmen and jackaroos would return to their paddocks, their horses loaded down with foodstuffs and other supplies. There were a few that were short supplies since they were waiting on the large shipment that was due shortly.

A few of the stockmen were confused, as Mel had them replace the people she wanted gone. Others split flocks and moved to other areas that Mel and Peter had determined needed a smaller flock. Only two men refused to take their wives and children into the bush with a flock, and they were working off their time as they waited for the wagons to arrive with supplies to take them back to Menindee. Maybe they would go to other stations for work since they were no longer welcome on Lawrence Station.

It was a matter of weeks before the shearers were done with all the flocks, but suddenly all the hustle and bustle, the noise, the coarse language was over and they were gone—down the road to another station

to do it all over again. They were paid in wool and some cash money for their hard work, promising to see Lawrence next year.

"That was something to see," Abigail admitted as they sat on the front porch the evening after the shearers left. She was overwhelmed by the amount of work that had just passed through the home paddock. The outsized buildings made sense to her now, as the scale of the operation came into focus. She was surprised to see Mel take out a pipe, crumble some leaf into the bowl, and light it. A pleasant aroma arose from the tobacco leaf, but to see what she knew was actually a woman smoking a pipe startled her. And then, Mel handed the pipe to her wife who sucked on the stem equally as hard, seeming to enjoy watching the puffs of smoke that came out of her mouth and drifted out of her nose.

"I thought as a mill owner you should see the entire process," Mel teased her as she watched Ainia gently touch the magpie chick. Its colors hadn't come in yet. It was kind of ugly at this stage, but it was alive and, for that, she was grateful. That, and sharing it with the children, who were all fascinated by the bird.

"The wagons should be here shortly," she reminded her friend, not because she wanted to get rid of her, but she wanted to provide her with options and a timetable. She glanced at her wife, pleased that she had been feeding Mack herself, no longer needing help with that chore or for Mel to carry her to the porch. Kug had returned to the village, but Mel had to go along with her to explain to her headman and former mate that they weren't returning her because they hadn't bought her, only hired her to help with the baby. It was very confusing to these people, and Alinta had to explain to the headman much better than Mel could.

"I learned a lot more about the process. I was so naïve," Abigail admitted, frowning as she thought about the letters she now wanted to

write. She hadn't realized everything involved in raising sheep and realized she had to rethink a lot of things for her businesses. It had actually shocked her how dirty the business of raising and sheering sheep was and she could go without seeing another season of birthing, remembering with a shudder the hands that had to go inside a sheep to help with some of the multiple-births and other problems that arose. She'd never heard of a prolapsed uterus before and hoped she wouldn't ever again. She'd watched as the stockmen, Mel included had mulesed and docked the sheep. Abigail had been horrified at the blood. She'd nearly fainted when one of the men, in an attempt to impress the countess had left off using his knife to make the cuts and instead used his teeth. The men also notched the ears of the wethers, making them easily identifiable after they had castrated the excess of males.

Mel smiled. "It's a dusty, dirty business," she agreed. Some of the men were still cleaning out the corners of the shearing shed, but it was hard to do, with all the bales waiting for the carts and wagons that to be offloaded here at the station and then loaded with the many large and heavy bales to return to Menindee, before being transferred onto the paddlewheel boats that would then take them to ships bound for England. In just the past couple of years, they had stopped taking it all the way back to Sydney across land and, instead, used Menindee as a shipping point. The drovers would herd their cattle or flocks of sheep onto these paddlewheel boats, too, as moving them was much easier by river, rather than across the vast land of the outback.

"I'd still like to meet your neighbors." She indicated in the direction of Twin Station south of them. She made it sound like they were just next door. "I want to meet and talk to this Mrs. Pearson about her horses."

Mel smiled. With the sheep now sheered, she had more free time and would be able to accompany her friend south, but not until her supplies had arrived. After equipping her various paddocks, the home paddock had nearly been cleaned out. In fact, they were out of some items, and her men would simply have to do without until the new items came in. They would be resupplied as Mel or Peter or anyone else who went to check on each of the paddocks brought them further supplies.

The three of them had talked about this before. Mel was reluctant to leave Alinta, but her wife encouraged her to go, certain she could ride with them. But Mel wasn't quite as enthused about that idea. The stitches had finally come out, and it had been uncomfortable for Alinta. Not only had they been uncertain when they should come out, but the first few times she had peed when they were in had been very painful for the woman. They stung each time for a long time, and rebuilding her blood supply since her great loss had taken so very long. Mel had given her a lot of hearty broths, having the kitchen staff kill chickens and make beef stew time and again to keep her well-supplied with it. Kug had gone out and found plants that had beaten anything the white people could have used for pain or antiseptic, and this, more than anything, had helped the woman heal from her ordeal. She wouldn't be having any more children, and they were both relieved because they had nearly lost her over this one.

"See more Diablo sibling," Alinta pidgeoned. "Dancer papa."

Abigail smiled, wanting to see this famous stud and see the other colts and fillies he might have sired. Maybe she would acquire one or two herself if Mrs. Pearson could be persuaded to part with a foal or two. Mel had told her the story about when they both left Sydney with their people, the large flock of Merino sheep, and the incredible impression this herd of black horses had made. She wanted to see it herself.

"Lawrence!" a voice called, infringing on their family time. Mel, sucking on her pipe once again, looked up to see Charley, their retired stockman with a gimpy leg, limping up rapidly to the porch.

"Hey, Charley. What can I do you for?" Mel called, rising up from her chair to lean over the porch rail.

"A lone rider came up and said the wagons are a day down the trail. They had trouble at one of the crossings, and a wagon tipped. They managed to retrieve most of its contents, but it delayed them."

Mel nodded thoughtfully, wondering what they had lost. She determined they would go over the manifest carefully. Sometimes these shipping companies had dishonest people working for them, and it wouldn't be the first time that an 'accident' occurred and some merchandise disappeared. "Feed him up and send him back," she said with a grin.

"Yup, he's already eatin' outta house and home," Charley quipped, returning the grin. He was looking forward to having a full shed of supplies to sort and inventory. It had been getting so he had to clean the dust from his shelves. He handled all the supplies for Lawrence Station for Mel and appreciated the job since he wasn't much good for anything else now with his gimpy leg. Lawrence had the utmost faith in him, and Charley appreciated the trust.

"Make sure you check their inventory with a fine-tooth comb when they get here, Charley," Mel said meaningfully and exchanged a knowing look with the storekeeper.

Charley saluted Mel respectfully and headed back down the path.

"Why does he limp, Papa?" Ainia asked as Mel sat back down and put the magpie the children had been feeding back in the cage.

"I think he had an accident at some point and hurt his leg. It's not polite to stare or ask someone why they limp," she advised conversationally. She didn't want to admonish the child, but she knew the other children who were enjoying the porch with the adults were listening, too.

"Bet it hurt," Agatha mentioned, poking her finger in the cage as the magpie chirped and then turned its head so she could rub. She smiled at the little bird.

"Look at that," Abigail said, pointing at the adult magpies watching them with the caged baby.

The twins, Augustus and Melbourne, were avidly watching the adult magpies with their black and white feathers. The birds seemed equally enraptured by all the small humans, watching the adults with some suspicion.

"We seem to be attracting an audience," Mel stated, amused at the funny birds. She noticed some of the birds weren't much older than the one they had in the cage, juvenile magpies. They were loud, friendly, and mischievous. As they waited for the supply train over the coming days, she watched as the juveniles played on the clothesline, driving the maids crazy. They weren't malicious, but any stray string or thread on the clothes was fair game. There always seemed to be one hanging upside down, and the others would pull at its feathers or legs, if they didn't have a string to pull on.

Mel took some of the baby toys out, and it was like the juvenile magpies had just been waiting for this. As they played with the toys, picking them up, and moving them around the yard, the children were enchanted watching them. Mel released their own baby bird, but it was too small and got picked, so she had to return it to the cage. It didn't stop

the show, though, as the children kept watching the young birds play. Some of the stockmen's children and even the village children were invited to play up at the big house and watched the many birds. They seemed to know they were being watched, and they showed off for their audience. More and more magpies came, bringing friends. It really got quite noisy with all the birds of various ages and personalities.

"Those are really smart birds," Mel declared as the other adults enjoyed the distraction. Mel hated that she had to get to work, but she found the adult birds seemed to recognize her and one or two followed her everywhere around the home paddocks. When she returned for lunch, she had to insist that the children eat their own lunches and then nap afterwards. If they argued, she threatened they couldn't play with the birds anymore. She counted as she ate, seeing there were at least two dozen magpies in various stages of growth, but none as small as the one they had in the cage. She fed this one the scraps from her plate. She looked up at the nest and saw its siblings watching them.

"They are going to dive down on us," Abigail worried as she watched these amazing birds. She'd never noticed birds before, and there was nothing like these back in England. It had happened so quickly, Mel's raising of this one and everyone noticing the rest. They were really quite fascinating.

"No, I think they find us as interesting as we find them."

"Funny bird," Ainia said as she leaned over Mack, hiding him from the birds' view as she ate her own lunch.

"They are funny birds," Mel agreed, grinning at their antics and knowing why the children hadn't wanted to go in to their naps.

All too soon, Mel had to go back to work. She'd spotted the dust cloud that indicated many carts and wagons were arriving here at the home

station. The oxen and bullocks pulling them had to be allotted paddocks, and, as the merchandise was carted off to the stockrooms and counted by Charley and his assistant, it was double-checked by Peter.

"Mr. Lawrence, sir?" A man approached her and doffed his hat. "I'm to personally deliver my wagonload to you," he said when she nodded to acknowledge him.

"Oh, and why is that?" she asked, astonished at his American accent.

"I have brought you cases of guns and ammunition from a ship that docked in Sydney. I was to personally escort them to you because of the amount you ordered and to make sure I handed them over to you myself." He handed Mel a letter that had accompanied the shipment. "The next shipment will come up the river on a paddleboat instead of being shipped overland," he informed her, looking at the fellow American curiously. He wondered how the man ended up so far in the outback. He'd been traveling for months to get his wagon out here, only to find out about the paddleboats and this cavalcade of merchandise heading for the Lawrence Station. It really was fortuitous to have joined up with them; it had been quite trying traveling on his own with this valuable consignment. There were too few people and too much vacant land, it had been unnerving at times.

"I've been waiting years for this shipment. You say there *will* be a second shipment?" she asked, astonished as she started walking for his wagon. "I thought for sure they had been stolen."

"It took a while, but we got them here," he said with a grin for the big man.

Mel looked in the wagon, astonished at the crates containing the repeating rifles she had ordered so long ago. She pulled herself up inside and held out her hand for the key to the lock. The man handed it to her,

and she unlocked it. Opening up the crate, she saw the guns were well-wrapped in oilskins beneath a padding of curls of wood that was inches deep. She slowly pulled a rifle through the inches and began to unwrap it. It was shiny and slick. Taking her red handkerchief, she began to rub the oil away from the stock of the barrel. She loved the look of the piece, and a wide smile spread across her face. She lay the weapon across her thighs and locked the crate back up. Standing up, she called out to Charley. She looked around for her store man and saw his limp before she saw the man.

"Yes, sir?" Charley called back, anxious to get back to his storehouse and to the counting.

"Have a couple of men unload these wagons at the house, and take these crates inside for me?"

"Yes, sir," he agreed, but he was annoyed at the interruption until Mel told him what was in them.

"I don't want them in the storerooms, as I want to make sure these guns go to people we know we can trust. They are extremely valuable, and I don't want random stockmen making off with them. You hear me?"

He understood. Repeating rifles in a place where single-action muskets were the norm, would make many a man foolish.

Right off, Mel gave one to Charley and one to Peter. They would slowly dole them out to the other stockmen, but only after a clear understanding that the guns were the property of Lawrence Station. In fact, Mel had the blacksmith make a brand that could be put on the stocks of each of the rifles, as well as the hand-guns stating their ownership. She wouldn't let any others out of the house except those she gave as gifts. The kegs and boxes of bullets were stored elsewhere, and she moved them after the men put the many shipping containers in her basement. She hid them within the big house.

Mel moved the guns up into the attic in a clean and dry area, knowing that the dampness of the cellar, where metal could rust, was no place for these items. She had only asked the men to put them down in the cellar because they would see the new guns and gossip would travel. Lawrence station now had a quantity of repeating rifles, and men would be envious. They would want these precious items for themselves over the muskets that were so common, and yet not so common … hard to come by and expensive to the men.

Mel kept one loaded on pegs over her front door, where she could grab it in a hurry if she needed it. She showed it to both Alinta and Abigail, teaching them how to load it after cleaning all the grease off it, how to dismantle it, and how to fire it. They had enough ammunition, with more on the way, that they could each practice shooting it to get a feel for handling and aiming it.

Once the supplies were all put away and the bales loaded on the wagons, several men were tasked with taking supplies to the outlying paddocks.

Mel took Alinta and Abigail out to practice. They soon had a crowd of men, women, and children watching. Mel allowed each of the adults and older children to get turns with the precious and valuable rifles.

"It was a good crop," Mel said as Alinta joined her for a walk, wearing Mack in a sling across her front. and Ainia holding Mel's hand.

"Crop?" she asked, confused. A crop was a piece of leather that made a short type of whip. Mel had explained this to her long ago.

"A crop is also something you grow, like food or the wool on the sheep's backs," she explained, smiling at the confusion it caused her wife. Mel stopped to admire the prosperous station she was so proud of, pleased that despite the hard birth, her wife and child were here with her. As she

stood there looking around, the ever-present magpies, noisy as ever, were following. One of them even got brave enough to land on Mel's arm as she leaned against the top rail of the paddock fence to inspect the saddle horses contained within. She froze and gazed in wonder at the bird up close as it examined her, both equally curious. She relaxed and was shocked when another landed on her other arm. They cawed at each other and then looked at Mel for her reaction. She just watched the two birds, amazed at how tame they'd become.

Alinta smiled at her wife, knowing she was special. She glanced down at Mack, who made sucking sounds in his sleep, and then down at her daughter, who was watching the birds on her father's arms in awe. She glanced around to see several employees were watching her husband, astonished and amused. She returned their smiles, remembering when she thought these grimaces were a danger. The birds finally hopped off and onto the rails and continued to watch the little family, as Mel put her arm around Alinta and they walked away.

OUTBACK FUTURE

CHAPTER TWELVE

Mel helped load the wagons they were taking to go to Twin Station so that Abigail could visit Carmen Pearson. The things Abigail had brought were well-packed in the wagons.

Mel was going to miss Auggie and Little Mel, as they had begun calling him. The twins were getting to such a delightful age. She looked forward to when Mack would be just as mischievous, inquiring, and talkative. She wouldn't rush it, though; he was perfect the way he was. She glanced to where Alinta was sitting on the porch, watching the wagons being packed and rocking the babe to sleep after having fed him.

Brodie, Bonnie, Leesa, and Leesa's son, Joseph, all got in the wagon, where Abigail's children and their servants were already loaded. Abigail rode alongside the wagons with her personal guard, ensuring she would eventually get back to Sydney in one piece. They would be leaving from

Twin Station and taking the paddleboat from Menindee down the river, then back to Sydney, and this would save them weeks, possibly months, of travel. This would be a big difference from their treacherous adventure across the outback and out to the Lawrence Station. During their stay, the guardsmen had undergone a complete change in style from their previous uniformed outfits, and each now looked like a man of the outback, with their pants made of thick cloth to protect them from the brush, an open necked shirt to allow them to cool off, and a brimmed bushman's hat to keep out the hot outback sun.

"Well, at least you won't be traveling at the end of summer," Mel commiserated with Abigail as they rode along.

Two wagons were behind them: one carrying the children, the nurses, and her wife and another, their supplies. Mel wouldn't let Alinta ride yet, and she had Mack with her. Ainia was playing with Abigail's children while she still could. Mel had sold Abigail several of her rifles for her guards, as well as a pistol, and a rifle for herself. She had also brought more rifles and ammunition to show her neighbors, Carmen and Fabiola, the owners of Twin Station, guessing they would likely want ones for themselves.

Abigail had written many letters and sent them off with the shipping foreman to be mailed from Menindee. She wished she had thought to send them sooner, but so much had happened since she got to Lawrence Station that she hadn't thought to send them until now. She'd spent several nights hurriedly writing to her lawyers, both here in Australia and in England, her shipping factory, her captain, and a slew of other people that she needed to receive answers from. She hoped she would hear replies on the more pressing arrangements by the time she got back to Sydney. She knew there was probably a stack of mail waiting for her there already from the

many months she had spent traveling into the outback, as well as staying at Lawrence Station.

She knew that Sir Boardman, her friend, lawyer, and estate manager in England, would be concerned. She hadn't consulted him when she had fled England and come to Australia; she had just told him what she was doing. Only, he had thought she was going to Belgium, and onto the rest of the continent. Instead, she had directed her captain, a Captain Scott, to plan for a further trip—all the way to Australia. She had written Boardman when she first arrived in Australia, but she hadn't stayed in Sydney long enough for a reply, instead, coming deep into the outback to see Melissa, now Mel. He would be worried; she was sure. She had so much to tell him, but, of course, there were many of the things about Mel she couldn't ever tell him.

She arranged for certain horses to be sent out from her various farms, knowing it would be months before she saw them and hoping they would cross the ocean safely. She already knew she intended to stay in Australia. It was safer than going back to England. She would have Captain Scott pretend he was taking the horses to Europe to sell for her in hopes that any spy her father had in her stables would fall for the ruse. She was certain the servants who had chosen not to go to Australia had talked, and her father had learned she had gone to Australia. She wanted Sir Boardman to spread a rumor she had gone from Australia to San Francisco and the western side of the United States. Maybe that would confuse him if he had sent anyone to Australia to find her. After all, she wasn't in Sydney, anymore. She didn't think her father had the money to send someone to kidnap her and her children, but she wanted to confuse him by throwing rumor after rumor his way.

She sent letters to her banker in Sydney, even her servants attending her horses there, and another to her solicitor, Mr. Saunders, in order to make sure they got the letters and that someone could read them aloud if they could not. She hoped she hadn't forgotten anyone. In fact, she'd written to some people more than once, as she thought of other things to tell them or ask them. She assured them all that she was doing well, that her children were happy and healthy, and gave some of them her itinerary as far as she knew it.

Mel had handed a packet of letters to the shipping foreman, as well, well wrapped in oil-skins and ready to hand off to the postmaster. With the paddleboats on the river, she wondered if post would move faster. She placed a third order with the gun supplier for more rifles, pistols, and tripled the amount of ammunition. She also wondered if the gun supplier thought she was going to start a war over here, but she knew when word got out, she could sell a lot of the guns for much more than it had cost her to import them. She also knew some would go missing over time and she wanted to be well-supplied. Knowing how long it had taken, the years it had taken to get this first order, she wanted to make sure they would have a steady supply of ammunition. There weren't a lot of guns like this, but the couple boxes she had now would engender gossip that would always make those who speculated on the amount think there were more than there actually was.

Mel also wrote her bankers around the world. She knew many of them by name, and, while most knew her as Melissa Lawrence, the ones in Sydney had met Melissa Lawrence, but also knew Mel Lawrence as her brother who had joined her in the outback to help her make a success of the large station. She laughed at this tiny ruse. Someday, such things wouldn't matter, but probably not in her lifetime. She also wrote her

business partner in Sydney, the dressmaker she had helped set up, informing her that Lady Worthington would be making her acquaintance when she returned to the city. Would she accommodate her friend? She was certain the dressmaker would be happy to assist someone of Abigail's position, the title alone would help the business.

Abigail had been quite amused that Mel owned shares in a dress shop but thought it quite practical. She remembered when they had traveled with Mel's father, and he had gifted her a dress. She had been so jealous of Mel and the shop owner, who had spent intimate time with Mel. In a way, her jealousy had become a blessing; it was how she had realized Melissa was a woman lover and that she herself wanted to be with her.

Alinta was pleased to be going along on the trip. She still napped a lot, but that was due to the needs of Mack and her body, as it continued to heal. The fact that she was young and healthy was very much in her favor. The stitches were long gone, and she was grateful, as they had itched horribly. The pull against her delicate skin had been unfamiliar, but she had talked Kug into finding certain plants and they had made a paste that helped with the healing of the torn skin. Mel had finally cut the stitches, and Alinta had been most relieved. The tugging of the knots had been uncomfortable, actually quite painful, and she'd been concerned at the drops of blood, but Mel assured her the skin was healed. They were both grateful she only had her normal flow and no other bleeding since then.

Alinta watched as Ainia played with the other children, knowing she would miss these friends who had lived with them these many months. There were other children at the home station, but it wouldn't be the same.

Mack was too young to play with, even though he was already alert and looking around, wide eyed in wonderment at this world he had been born into. Soon enough he would sit up, then stand up and be following his sister.

Alinta recognized certain landmarks and eagerly looked forward to seeing Carmen and Fabiola. Not so much Harold, Fabiola's brother, as the man always seemed odd to her. He wasn't like the men on their own station or even others at Twin Station. The man gave her an odd feeling, as though she couldn't trust him. She knew Mel felt the same way about him. Carmen and Fabiola made up for it, though. They were genuinely pleasant to her and had earned her friendship over the years.

For Mel's part, the wagons seemed to travel especially slow as they headed south. When they had to pass through the newly constructed gates to get on Twin Station land from Lawrence Station, she was pleased to see the fencing operation had completed this section. She liked the definitive break between the lands, knowing that what she had claimed and what others claimed was now demarcated by the fencing. They climbed the hills to Twin Station and set off across its vast miles, seeing very few stockmen as they, too, had just returned from their home station, where their sheep had been sheared. Mel unconsciously made mental counts of the sheep she saw and the number of lambs.

"Whew, you were not joking when you said it was a long ride," Abigail said, as they climbed another set of hills. The roads weren't the best for the wagons, and Mel had said it probably would have been better with carts, but for the children and supplies they were taking. Abigail and her

party needed to have enough to get them safely back to Menindee, as well as take their things home with them.

"It's not so bad," Mel answered, amused. The Englishwoman had changed a lot over the past months. She no longer wore her English dress clothes, but rather stockmen's outfits, much to the shock and dismay of her maid Brodie. The girl simply didn't have much to do since Abigail started wearing the simpler clothes, without skirts or corsets.

"Well, I'm glad you both came along, or I'd have been quite lost without you." Abigail realized that Australia was so much larger than anyone knew. The small part she had seen had been incredibly vast. It boggled the mind, but she was so happy she had done it, now. She had acquired some knowledge of the terrain, some of its people, and many animals that couldn't have been explained without experiencing them. She'd also grown up a lot in ways she didn't know she had needed.

Mel smiled. She was glad she had included Alinta. It had been a long set of months since Abigail had arrived with her declaration of love. Alinta had trusted her to deal with the situation and had even befriended the intruder. She glanced over at her wife, who was watching them from the wagon, listening to the conversation out of curiosity, not mistrust. She turned that smile towards the woman she loved, pleased when her wife returned it. Suddenly, Alinta stopped smiling and pointed ahead on the trail. She and Mel both looked, catching her breath.

"Abigail, look!" she pointed and the Englishwoman too gasped.

In the distance on the broad plain before them, there was a sight few could say they had ever seen. There were dozens of black horses galloping through the grasses, stretched out, their manes and tails flying in the breeze. No one was chasing them; they were running for the sheer joy of

being alive. Several had smaller foals, in various stages of growth, following along behind.

Mel looked closer and, as they drew closer, could see a few specks that became vaqueros, waving their sombreros at her and her wife, as they recognized the owner of Lawrence Station. She turned her attention back to the horses, the beauty that was the blacks. "I didn't lie now, did I?" she murmured to Abigail, who seemed to have died and gone to heaven.

"You did not," she admitted weakly. She'd been impressed by Diablo, but he was almost a pale imitation to the enormity of what she was now seeing. She saw more than one stallion in this mixed herd. She realized that they were young, like Diablo, and would soon either be sold or castrated. The visual effect of the herd though wasn't lost on her, either, and she would never have allowed her Thoroughbreds to run like this, fearing severe injury or death from the uneven ground. The freedom these animals were showing, the absolute lack of fear, the joy as they galloped along, was something she wanted bred into her own animals.

Mel laughed at her friend, amused because she could so easily read her mind. She, too, had felt that way when she saw the blacks, but seeing them in this open range was different. They looked wild and free, untamed and wonderful.

Alinta turned away from the horses and watched as Mel and then Abigail saw the herd. She remembered not so very long ago when such animals would have meant meat to her and her people. She hadn't ever seen them before she met white men, but she now appreciated the beauty before her. She saw the wonderment on her wife's face and the absolute delight. Now, she understood why Mel was so pleased to own Diablo. She herself had gone out to say goodbye to the animal, and it was like he had known and was depressed she was going away. She hadn't known

that an animal could feel such affection for a human. He had returned to his valley looking a little dejected, and Alinta had felt bad leaving the animal. She had never known that feeling for an animal, either.

They slowly passed the herd, Alinta, Mel, and Abigail lost in thoughts of their own but watching the beautiful blacks the entire time. The children watched them for a brief moment, before losing interest and turning back to each other for entertainment.

It took another day to get to the home station, and when they did, Fabiola and Carmen were away inspecting their southern paddocks. Mel explained that it had all burned years ago in a raging fire and that Carmen's sheep had helped to restock the station. There was no sign of Harold, and, for that, Mel was grateful. The man was just too unsettling. She couldn't even really explain why. He was always watching when he was about, but something about his gaze was shifty, weak, and made her uncomfortable.

The visitors were put up in houses reserved for stockmen with families, and Mel looked up the hill to what was now Carmen's finished hacienda. She'd ride up there later after they were all settled and see it. She was fascinated to see a hacienda in the middle of the outback. She'd only ever seen those in California when she had been there briefly.

"You say this station is older than yours?" Abigail asked Mel as they walked around, her tone disparaging. Alinta was taking a nap with Mack, while Bonnie, Leesa, and Brodie kept the other children amused. The children had napped in the wagons on the way here and were bursting with energy. Employees of the station had put them all up in vacant houses kept for these visitors when stockmen with families weren't using them. The children were eyeing the strange children of the stockmen on this new station and the Aboriginal village down by the creek.

"Shhh," Mel warned her, knowing if she unintentionally said something insulting that she wouldn't make a favorable impression on Carmen and certainly not on Fabiola. "Yes, their station is decades older. It was settled by Carmen's uncle and Fabiola and Harold's father." She went on to explain that the men had been from England, good friends, some thought cousins. Fabiola's father had gone to America and married a Hispanic woman, producing the daughter that inherited her share of the station from her uncle.

Lowering her voice to a whisper, Abigail said, "They could learn a few things from your station."

Mel was pleased but didn't show it. She wondered about the newer hacienda and how much Carmen had been able to influence Fabiola, who hadn't wanted too much change. She understood that some of the way Fabiola and Harold did things was out of habit, the way things were always done, but it didn't mean they wouldn't change. She hoped Carmen would influence them into making some improvements. She knew that money had been tight, especially with a fire that had wiped out their southern paddocks and that great loss of sheep.

After their long trip, the visitors ate supper in their separate houses, and everyone went to bed early. The guards slept in the wagons near the houses where Abigail and her children were. Mel was amused, to see them take turns guarding the wagons and the house. She was up a few times helping Alinta with Mack and watched them watching the house. They were taking their duties seriously. She wondered if they would ever again wear the uniforms of the Worthington family, or would they prefer the stockmen's garb they had been wearing for the last few months. It was more comfortable, and the dirt didn't cling like it did on the other attire. It was far less noticeable, too, she'd be sure to mention that to Abigail who

might or might not want her guards conspicuous back in Sydney. Mel also noticed they had all cleaned and shined up their new rifles and pistols, their latest new and valuable pieces of equipment.

Mel slept soundly through the early morning and was up as the sun made an appearance over the horizon. Alinta enjoyed cooking again, remembering the times when Mel taught her. She fried rashers of bacon along with some fresh eggs one of the stockmen had brought her, and they ate their breakfast while she nursed Mack and Mel helped Ainia with her plate of food.

Mel was pleased to see Fabiola and Carmen return later that morning. Every time she had started to head up to hacienda, she had been distracted by something. Now, she had an excuse to go see the fabulous house Carmen had built. The same man, Shamus O'Grady, had built the hacienda and then come north to build the house and then the great barns for Mel.

"Well, well, well, look what the cat dragged in," Fabiola teased, pleased to see her neighbor as she slid from her Brumby and gave the big man a hug.

Surprised, Mel returned the hug, before being handed off to Carmen, who also hugged her and gave her a kiss on both cheeks. "I'm so pleased you are here," she said, her slight Hispanic accent endearing to Mel's ears.

Abigail saw the slight brush on Mel's face and looked at the reason for it. Carmen Pearson was not what she had expected at all. She was pretty, with her black eyes and long, curly, brown hair—dark, almost black. Her stride wasn't very feminine, but it had a confidence in it Abigail hoped she would have someday. She hadn't expected a Hispanic woman with the name Pearson, but then Mel hadn't given her the woman's full name before.

"Senora Carmen Valenzuela Pearson, I would like you to meet Lady Abigail Worthington," Mel introduced them and smiled as she saw the clashing of cultures.

Carmen's eyebrows shot up at being introduced to a lady, and Abigail smiled at the pretty Mexican woman. Neither was what the other expected.

CHAPTER THIRTEEN

Carmen was thrilled to find another woman who loved horses as much as she did and showed off the hacienda first. It spread out over the terrace it was built upon, with stables on lower terraces, gardens, and an abundant array of flowers everywhere.

"How are you going to keep those gardens and flowers in the hot outback sun?" Mel asked, having lived through a few summers out here.

"My men found a cave that we dug into and found an aquifer," she explained, "and the water that seeped into where they dug did not evaporate right away. It lasts long enough to supply us with plenty of fresh water. We filled our barrels," she nodded towards the large structures on legs that dotted the landscape down at the main yard, built long ago by Fabiola and Harold's father and her own uncle. "And we have a few up here, in case," she indicated a few hidden in the rocks of the hill

she had built upon. "The men have been building holding dams, hiding them with the terraces so we can keep some water on the land." She explained how they intended to build more, further out, for their stock. Mel was fascinated, intending to learn more so she could do that on her own station.

They all exclaimed over the coolness of the hacienda, built with native stone and mud that was baked by the hot sun.

"My people would be proud," she proclaimed, referencing her Californio and Mexican-Spanish heritage. "The Aboriginals here helped us find the water so we could build up here," she stated, giving them credit. "A couple of my vaqueros have taken wives from the village. We built a village on the far side." She showed them the adobe style huts of many rooms, larger than the huts that Mel had observed in California. "I want them to have homes," she explained. "You know, one of my people returned to California?"

Mel nodded, having remembered that not everyone was suited for the great outback. It did funny things to some people, turning their mental well-being. Others thrived, and still others simply made due.

"I've written for a teacher, and we'll have school here." She indicated a building that was in progress on one of the terraces.

"A church, too?" Mel asked, remembering the pompous man who had married her to Alinta and made so many assumptions.

"Well, I suppose it could be used for that as well, but I didn't write the church for a teacher. I don't want the children of my people or my children to have some of that rhetoric instilled in them. I'd rather they make up their own minds. The occasional traveling cleric can hold a service if he is so inclined, but I won't offer a position to any of them permanently."

"They make too many rules," Fabiola put in, having accompanied them on the tour of the hacienda and terraces. "They weren't here while we built up the place, but they want to dictate to our people how they should live and take their tithe?"

Mel understood that and had been of a similar opinion. She had to find out where Carmen had written, as she would do the same, offering a position to a teacher who would be willing to teach her children, her stockmen's children, and even any of the Aboriginal children whose parents would allow it. She knew that they needed to learn the white man's ways, even if she hated the idea that it would change their village life for all time. There was no changing the fact that whites were here and would be changing the way things were done. She would give their children a chance, too, and, if any of the people she hired were prejudiced, they would be the ones to go, not the people whose lands these belonged to at one time.

It was the stables, though, that made Mel and Abigail ecstatic. They were almost as big as the barns that Mel had built. These two were of an adobe and native rock design with large sleepers on top of the stones. This would keep bugs that ate wood from destroying the wooden and adobe structures. The insides were made of rich wood and luxurious, a great environment for the horses Carmen was raising to have room to grow as her herd increased.

"We would hire the Irishman back, but he seems to have disappeared back to Sydney," Fabiola told them.

"He probably disappeared there to drink away all his money," Mel said wisely. "I made sure he paid his men before he left after building at my place."

"I did that, too," Carmen mentioned, but she quickly looked down, distracted by Mack, whom she had taken from Alinta upon first sight. She cooed and entertained him, while Alinta held Ainia's hand to keep her from exploring the horse stalls too closely.

"This is marvelous!" Abigail exclaimed, running her fingers along the sanded wood, feeling how the shiny wood had been tended carefully and wondering at it. There were no bite marks from fractious horses, but there were single stalls for horses, as well as box stalls for various purposes. She could see into one where a mare was watching them, her foal sucking enthusiastically at her teat. "Oh, how precious!"

Carmen wasn't used to the British woman's accent and smiled her thanks at the compliment of one of her babies. The horses were doing wonderfully well out here. Parts of the outback were not unlike the desert-like areas of California, where the Mustangs thrived. Carmen kept her men busy watching over her growing herd so her babies wouldn't go wild. Already Brumbies had been spotted, and she'd tasked a few of her people with capturing them, if they could. She thought, with judicious breeding, they could improve her strain of horses.

Mel, Abigail, and Carmen discussed breeding some of Carmen's horses with Abigail's Thoroughbreds and what the resulting offspring would be like. Fabiola had very little to contribute, and Alinta, nothing at all. Still, the two smiled and listened, learning a lot from the horse-crazy women. The talk continued into the evening, and Carmen offered the British woman, Mel and her wife, and all their children rooms in the hacienda. Although they appreciated the offer, they declined as they didn't want to move their things. It was late before everyone was in bed.

Mel, accustomed to being up early, was pleased to run into Fabiola as she walked up the hill to the hacienda.

"Good morning," Fabiola said pleasantly when she spotted the Yank. They were silent as they walked up the hill, using steps when they could, but also the zig zag of the terraces.

"Good morning," Carmen repeated when the two arrived, turning around abruptly from where she had been watching the sunrise on one of the terraces

"Good morning," Mel responded back to her.

In no time, they were discussing improvements on their respective places. Fabiola had already said she wanted to find the Irishman, but Mel suggested that she write to the ferryman in Menindee asking if he knew any other builders who would want some work.

"Why him?"

"That town is growing. I was down there a while back, and he knows everything and everyone who comes through there."

"That's smart," Carmen admitted. "We need to update some of the buildings. Some of them are as old as my uncle and their father were when they came out here."

Fabiola added, "We will need some new ones, too. Thanks to all those sheep you two brought out here, we need to expand for the flocks." She smiled at both of them in turn.

Mel had also noticed that, with them so near the creek that flooded each year, the spring would be miserable to deal with the water and mud that engendered. Her own buildings were on the side of the hill and had never been flooded. They still had the muck that many animals created, but it was easier to shovel downhill or spread it out on the fields they were cultivating.

They discussed crops and animals, Carmen asking after Diablo. Mel had forgotten to ask about Dancer, but she wasn't surprised to find he was out with the herd.

"Let's ride out to the herd today so you can see them," Carmen enthused.

In no time at all, they were all mounted, Alinta insisting on riding, despite Mel's worry about her healing.

"Long 'nough time. I heal," she insisted as she sat side-saddle on a horse that Fabiola arranged for her.

Ainia rode in front of Mel, and Carmen took her young daughter, Rachel, up before her. Mel was pleased to see Carmen's sons—Philippe, Sebastián, and Nicolás—all riding their own horses, following their mother as though they were vaqueros insisting on riding along with their group. When she had first met them, they were around 10, 7, and 5 respectfully, and while she knew they would grow older, it was a surprise to see how much they had aged. Time had gone by quickly.

"Well, if everyone else is bringing their children, I think Agatha could ride with me," Lady Abigail stated, smiling at seeing the group with children going out to the herd.

Agatha was thrilled to ride with her mother, her brothers seeming to get more attention normally. Seeing the other children with their mothers, she was only envious of the boys who had their own horses.

"We'll have to get a pony so you can practice when we get back to Sydney," Abigail murmured as she saw her daughter's envious look.

"Really?" she asked, amazed, looking up at her mother joyfully.

"Well, I think we should build our own place."

"Like this?" she indicated the hacienda as they descended along the paths that wove back and forth along the high hill.

"No, maybe something like back home, but uniquely ours. Something Australian," Abigail told her with a smile.

"So, you are settling in Australia for certain, then?" Fabiola asked, keeping an eye on Nicolás, the youngest of Carmen's sons who had a tendency to be a bit reckless, trying to keep up with his older brothers.

"I believe so. I don't think I want to live out here, despite the incredible spaces. I think I would do better closer to Sydney."

"Where exactly were you thinking?" Mel asked, moving her horse up closer to Abigail so she didn't have to raise her voice. Her arms surrounded Ainia, holding the little girl securely on the saddle.

"I was thinking how lovely some of those areas near to the Blue Mountains might be. It's still cool enough there that I won't die of the heat." She smiled as she indicated the hot outback they were riding through. It was still cool enough this time of year, although, so far, they hadn't reached the baking temperatures that were expected. "I think I might be able to buy some good lands around there."

"They'd probably give you some," Fabiola commented, glancing at the other two boys as she kept an eye on Nicolás.

"I think if you approached the governor, he might help you obtain just the right property," Carmen put in, thinking aloud. "You might want to be careful in how you approach anyone who settled there, or if it's still crown lands."

"Careful?" Abigail asked as they reached the bottom of the hill and set off across the vast station for the valley where Carmen had allowed her herd to roam. She saw now that some of the men were in the process of putting up fences, something she hadn't noticed coming in from the north and Mel's station.

"Once they know you are Lady Worthington, the price will go up," Mel explained. "You will need an intermediary and a few favors."

Used to a more settled area of the world, Abigail nodded thoughtfully. Still, she had essentially bribed officials to obtain a lordship for her second son. She understood the concept of greasing a few palms to get what she wanted.

"Now, all you have to decide is which side of the Blue Mountains you want to live on," Carmen teased, a dimple hinting at the corner of her cheek as she smiled.

Abigail laughed as she agreed. She had wanted to know about these black horses the Hispanic woman was raising, or she would have gone to Menindee and taken a paddleboat downstream to get to Sydney more quickly. She was glad she had traveled all this way from Lawrence Station to meet this woman and see her horses.

Mel surreptitiously watched her Hispanic friend, certain that Fabiola was courting Carmen. After all these years, she wouldn't be surprised if the two became more than cousins, although, technically, they weren't related. She knew, at one time, Fabiola had hoped that Carmen would marry her weak brother, Harold, but that notion only lived on in Harold's mind, now. No one else who knew Carmen would ever think of those two as marrying. Carmen already had four heirs, and, while neither Harold nor Fabiola had heirs, it was apparent that neither was in a hurry to provide one. Fabiola had no desire to ever be pregnant, much less raise a child of her own, and Harold, lacking in ambition, preferred living off the land his sister basically ran. He had gone along with the idea of marrying their

cousin, ensuring that the station they lived on would be theirs forever, but she had proven difficult to convince.

What Harold didn't realize was that Carmen was not interested in him and would never be interested in him. Because of her association with Mel, she realized that there were options that didn't involve adding another weak man to her life. She didn't need a man in order to run a ranch—or station, as they called them here in the Outback; she had Fabiola's excellent advice and her own instincts to develop the place. Her father had been a man of vision and had taught her much. She missed him after he was gone. She had learned much over the years and was still learning. She had brought her own livestock, including her beloved horses from America as well as the Merinos she had purchased in Sydney, and had her own people around her for comfort. She didn't want a man underfoot and preferred Fabiola's company, and the Australian woman could frequently be found heading up to the hacienda in the early mornings to have breakfast with the Californian.

As they came over the last rise, they saw the large herd before them, meandering about, searching out their favorite shady spots before the heat of the day would come and beat down upon them.

"They're beautiful!" Abigail breathed, and Agatha heard the note of awe in her mother's voice, finding an affinity with her over the stunning black horses.

"I can't see this enough," Mel agreed with her, pointing out foals to Ainia. She glanced at Alinta who returned her pleasurable smile. While she thought the horses were beautiful, too—so many that looked like her

beloved Diablo—she only now understood the affinity that a person could have with such an animal.

Carmen looked on with pride, waving at her Segundo, or foreman as they would call him in English, an actual distant cousin of hers, who was watching the herd and keeping them safe for her. He slowly rode his horse towards the rather large group that had come to see the herd.

"Buenos dias, senora," he said, taking the wide sombrero from his head in respect to Carmen.

"Paco, it's time to replace that dilapidated hat of yours. Take one from the storeroom," she ordered in a teasing tone.

"This one still has life," he defended the sombrero that had seen better days. He really hesitated to part with it. It was one of the last vestiges of California where he had been born and raised. He had been faithful to his employer and cousin Carmen, though, and followed her to Australia and the outback.

"Says the man with a hole in his hat," she teased and then glanced beyond him at the herd. "Anything new?"

"There is another stallion trying to move in, and Dancer challenged him," he reported, turning serious as he looked at the horses. "The Brumby tried to move in under the early morning darkness, but Dancer is too smart," he said pridefully. "I have two of my men tracking the Brumbies, and we will try to catch the Mustangs."

"Brumby? Mustang?" Agatha asked, confused. She had heard the names before at Mel's and needed clarification.

"A Brumby and a Mustang are the same thing," Mel explained, not only for the little countess's benefit, but so all the children would learn. "Brumby is Australian for a wild horse. Mustang is American, where I am from, for the same wild horse."

"There are wild horses besides these?" she indicated the black herd milling about in the bottom of the valley before them.

"These are not wild, mi chiquitín, my little one," Carmen gently corrected her, explaining her Spanish word at the same time. "These are my babies."

Agatha looked from the Hispanic woman to the black horses to the three children on their own horses to the little girl Rachel on the horse with her mother, confused. Carmen smiled back at her, noting the confusion.

"I raised these horses in California, and now they breed and live here. They are not wild. My cousin Paco, here," she pointed to the vaquero who had come up to tell them of the Brumbies, "says there are some wild horses that will try to steal my babies, and my stallion would have none of it." She spied Dancer eyeing her and her guests, his nose raised regally as he scented them on the wind, determining if they were friend or foe. It was that carriage of his that was part of his beauty.

"Is that Dancer, there?" Abigail asked, waving towards the stallion and catching her breath. She could see now why Diablo was so valuable. Although beautiful, he was a poor imitation of his sire who was in his prime, but the potential was there and Diablo could become just as great. She could see why Mel had wanted the handsome brute so much.

"Si, that is Dancer," Carmen agreed pridefully.

They watched for a while as the horses ambled about, and, finally, Carmen led their group down to the valley floor and dismounted to approach the stallion. Dancer pranced his way up to her, looking like he was going to run her down, with his tail swishing at flies and an intense look in his eyes. It caused many gasps from the children and Abigail who were watching, but he stopped in time so that Carmen could pet him and talk to him.

Abigail understood horse talk, but, whatever the Hispanic woman said to the stallion, she didn't understand Spanish. The body movements, though, told her that the woman and the horse had genuine affection for each other.

"She could have sold any of those horses for a lot of money on the way out here from Sydney," Mel explained.

"She has a hard time selling any of them," Fabiola responded, watching her friend and business partner. She was always amazed at the friendship between woman and beast.

"I'm grateful for Diablo. He will be a fine stud in years to come," Mel stated, looking at a couple of the mares thoughtfully.

"We need to get back to the home station," Carmen said as she released the stallion from her hug and slapped him on the flank to hurry him along back to his mares. "I have a mare ready to foal." Her eyes were suspiciously wet when she walked back to them. The adults pretended not to see it, but the children were not so subtle.

"Why are you crying, Mama?" Rachel asked as her mother got on the horse behind her. If the other children weren't aware of Carmen's tears, they all looked now.

"I miss my friend."

"But you come out here all the time to see him?"

"I know, and I love him," she admitted with a wry little grin.

Mel and Abigail could understand that; they'd each had their favorite horses over the years. Abigail waited until they were on their way once again before she brought up the horse breeding they had discussed the night before. "I'd like to send you a couple of mares to breed to Dancer, but would you let me have one of your foals?"

They went back and forth on the topic, and Carmen finally resigned herself to let some of the offspring of her horses go. After all, they couldn't interbreed with Dancer without losing some of the quality she had bred so judiciously all these years.

"I will want to breed a couple of my mares to one of your Thoroughbred stallions at some point," she countered.

Surprised, Abigail agreed but explained it would be several years before her home and stables were built, even though she'd already sent for some horses. It would be months before she received responses to her many letters and the horses would arrive. She hoped, by then, to have acquired the land and arranged to have stables built for them.

"You did?" Mel asked, joining in the conversation. "Which ones?"

Abigail told her the names of the horses, some of which Mel recognized as ones her own father had purchased years ago and some, Abigail explained, were offspring of those same horses.

Fabiola exchanged a commiserating look with Alinta who smiled to see how happy talking about horses made Mel. Alinta was learning about horses, listening as avidly as the children to understand her mate's enjoyment of the animal.

OUTBACK FUTURE

CHAPTER FOURTEEN

Mel and Alinta stayed at Twin Station much longer than they had planned, a full week with their friends, before heading north to accompany Abigail and her group to the turnoff leading to Menindee. Behind Abigail's wagon was tethered a black yearling filly and a young stallion she had negotiated from Carmen. Carmen and Fabiola rode with them for a way, under the guise of taking supplies to some of their eastern paddocks, but, really, they didn't want the visit to end so soon.

"I want to thank you for everything," Abigail said sincerely. As she said her goodbyes to Mel, she kept her tears at bay.

"Well, at least we are on the same continent now, and our letters won't take as long to arrive," Mel teasingly consoled her. "We have our horse breeding to focus on."

Abigail shook her head at her friend as she hugged her hard and, for a second, regretted that she had to move on. Mel had been her first love, her only love, and she didn't know what the future would hold. She had her children to raise as she saw fit, and she would soon have a station of her own to build, she hoped. Mel, Alinta, Carmen, and Fabiola had given her plenty of ideas and advice, and she eagerly looked forward to the challenges she'd face making her own way in this wild land. She took a deep breath, closed her eyes for a second, then looked over Mel's shoulder and into Alinta's ancient and knowing eyes. Releasing Mel was easier than she'd thought it would be, and she reached for a surprised Alinta.

"I need to thank you, too, for having me and my children. It's been a wonderful visit." And she meant it. She would miss this quiet and kind woman who had taught her a lot, as well.

"You come again," Alinta said, hugging her back, as she knew now that this was acceptable, even expected. She had learned a lot from this English woman, and she smiled as she stepped back. She looked on as the two women from Twin Station said their goodbyes to Mel, and then they followed suit with her. She had hugged the children, too, knowing she and Alinta, especially, would miss them all.

After admonishments to write, children crying, and lots of waving, the two parties loaded back up and went their separate ways.

After leaving Mel and Alinta as their wagon traveled north, the rest of the group, including some of the vaqueros and all of Abigail's guard, headed east, spending one last night out together as their talk centered around horses and sheep and the breeding of both. Carmen and Fabiola had been pleased to hear about the different kinds of sheep Mel had purchased; different breeds for different purposes, breeding with the Merinos she had started with. It led to some interesting conversations.

Carmen and Fabiola headed south to one of their remote paddocks to bring supplies to their stockmen, and Abigail's party headed further east, her two wagons, supplies, and stock well-guarded. Her men were a lot more confident after spending over a year out in the Outback guarding the dowager Countess Worthington, Abigail; her daughter, Lady Worthington; her twin sons Lord Worthington and Lord Brentford—as well as her servants, Bonnie and Charlotte; the nursemaids; and her personal maid, Brodie.

Abigail, Dowager Countess Worthington had a lot on her mind as she rode her horse east, ahead of the wagon that held her children, her maid's child, her maids, and all their supplies. She had a lot to plan for, and there would be no one to stop her; she wouldn't allow it.

Seeing Mel and how she lived with her wife had given her a lot of food for thought. Further, seeing Twin Station with Fabiola and Carmen and how they lived, she wondered if the two of them would ever be more than business partners and decided it didn't matter. They were happy with how things were, and, if they were intimate, that was no one's business but their own. Still, they lived respectfully in separate homes. She wondered at the absentee brother whom she hadn't seen during the entire week she had been there.

Seeing the grand house that Mel had built and the large but functional and beautiful hacienda Carmen had built, she wondered what kind of home she should build for her own family. She glanced back at the children, knowing they would miss their playmates they had become accustomed to for so long. She wondered what her own future would hold. She had so many ideas, and not just about the house and land she intended to acquire. She'd been gone from Sydney much longer than she had planned, and now was anxious to return, but only so she could leave it again and search for

land so she could build a grand home of her own, as well as extensive stables for the horses she intended to breed.

Abigail certainly hadn't thought her sojourn in the outback would end like this. She glanced back at the two blacks she had acquired, it had cost her a pretty penny and a few promises wrung out of the Californian, as well as a few she meted out of her own plans. She smiled in anticipation of the horses she would breed, the ones that Carmen would breed, and even Mel, who had her two herds started and had asked to acquire a few of the Thoroughbreds she had relinquished so long ago.

She thought back the many months ago when she had made this journey in the heat of summer and realized how foolish she had been. Seeing Mel in her element, she had grown to understand that all relationships move on if they aren't tended, and she had missed her chance. If she had left with Mel when she had asked all those years ago, her life would have been different—very, very different. Still, Mel was happy with Alinta, and she actually liked the woman and had learned so much from them both. But who was out there waiting for her? Would she find her someday, or was the countess meant to have friends only? Would she have to be content with building a life here in Australia and raising her children?

Abigail wasn't afraid of those questions. The outback had changed her, and she didn't mind the change. She felt ready to take on the world, and woe betide the man or woman who tried to stop her. She had the money at her fingertips to do what she wanted, and she wouldn't let anyone tell her differently.

As she sat around the fire nightly, her servants talking eagerly about what they would find in Sydney when they returned, she thought about her plans and expanded them in her mind.

"I'm sorry, mistress," Brodie told her, handing her the plate that contained her simple meal.

"For what?" Abigail asked, curious. The trip had been going well, and they were only two days out of Twin Station.

"That you never found your friend," she answered, frowning, her brogue becoming evident.

Abigail blinked, realizing that Brodie hadn't realized that Mel was the Melissa she had spoken of on their way out. Covering, she answered, "Well, her brother more than made up for it, and we learned a lot out here."

"I'll be glad to get back to civilization, though," the maid said agreeably. "There weren't much for me to do for you out here."

Abigail realized the woman thought she would be attending to the countess's dresses and finery once again, but, after having worn pants and then later a split skirt she had made at Mel's direction, she didn't think she would wear a dress unless she was going into town. She wondered if she would lose the nursemaids that took care of her sons and daughter, or if they would stay with her when she announced her plans. Were they too completely under the spell of Mel instead of the Melissa they had been expecting? Had they been fooled by Mel?

In the week it took to get to Menindee by wagon, arrange passage for everyone and their stock down the river, and find a ship that was going to Sydney. Abigail had mapped out her plans more clearly, the nearer they got to civilization. She was looking forward to staying in the house she had rented so long ago, and she was going to make the acquaintance of a few government officials Fabiola had recommended, including the governor, so she could get her plans for the next stage of her life started.

The site of the huge harbor engendered many of the travelers to send up a cheer. Abigail watched as her children joined in, despite not knowing why they were cheering. She remembered Mel telling of her own experiences on a ship, shuddering at the thought of being a virtual slave to those disgusting men.

She watched Dunbar Head slide by, followed by South Head, before they turned into the mile-wide harbor that was the entrance to Sydney Harbor. She saw the many inlets, islands, and what she was told were Middle, Georges, and Chowder Head, headlands that marked the large harbor.

She didn't know why, but this place almost, but not quite, felt like home to her, and she was relieved to see something familiar as they docked and she was able to unload her wagon and horses, to take them and her people to the house she had rented. She was in a temporary home, for now, and it was up to her to *make* a home for herself and her children. Abigail's future was here in Australia, and, while she wouldn't stay in Sydney, the outback—with all its stark beauty, struggles, and opportunity—awaited her.

If you have enjoyed **OUTBACK FUTURE**, I hope you will enjoy this excerpt from
VETTED AGAIN

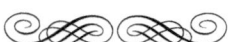

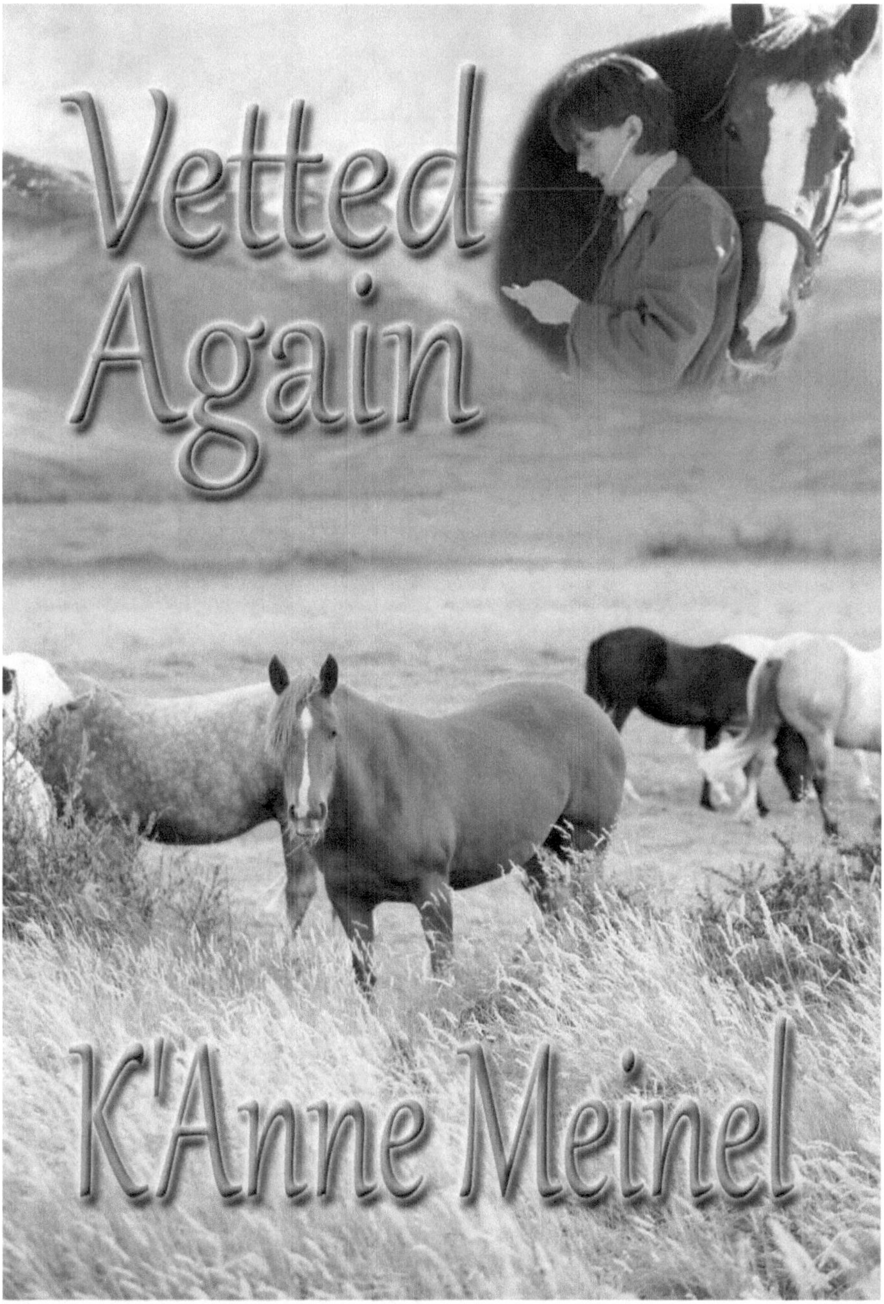

Herriot Family Tree

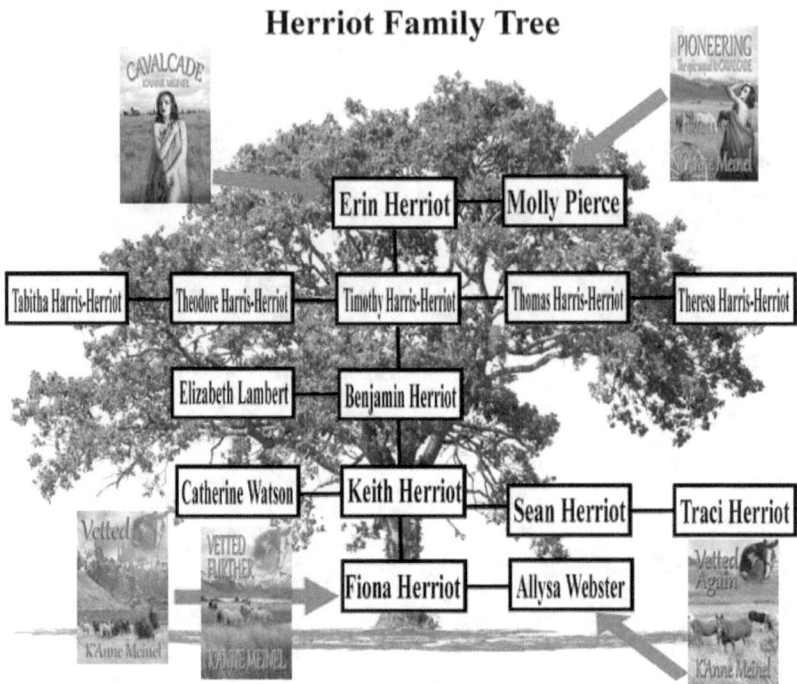

CHAPTER ONE

Allyssa didn't remember much about the ride back to the ranch. Their intended shopping trip was forgotten as Fiona rambled on and on about being pregnant together. Finally, sensing Allyssa's quiet and unease, Fiona pulled over at the end of their driveway and asked, "Are you okay? Aren't you happy about your pregnancy? This is what you *wanted*, isn't it?"

The shock was wearing off, and Allyssa stared unblinking at her wife for a moment as the sense of what she was saying began to penetrate. "Of course, this is what I *wanted*. I just thought it wasn't meant to be. When my test came up negative, I just accepted the result. I didn't think to question the result, and what if how I've been living— riding and going about my day as though I wasn't pregnant—has harmed the baby?" She suddenly touched her stomach wonderingly, remembering the feeling of being pregnant last year and knowing this was completely different.

"You are awfully quiet," Fey pointed out gently, worrying about Allyssa and her mood swings.

"I just realized…How in the world are we going to cope with two babies at the same time?"

"Just like any other new parents of twins cope with two babies, I guess."

"They won't be twins," she pointed out. She worried about all the complications they could face when the babies were born, but Leslie had assured her she was healthy and the pregnancy progressing normally. She had also explained that no two pregnancies were the same, and Allyssa needed to take care of herself, not only because of what had happened the previous year but also because of her activities on the ranch. She had given her some prenatal vitamin samples and a prescription for more.

"They are not considered twins because we are each carrying one, but they are from the same daddy, so brother or sister or both are going to be raised as though they were twins," Fiona pointed out in return. She had gone along with the double implantation for the sake of her wife's well-being but really hadn't thought both would take. She'd humored Allyssa and now, look at them. They were both pregnant. She wondered if their health insurance company would be suspicious.

"That's true," Allyssa fretted, sounding distinctly unhappy.

"It's a little late to change your mind," she tried teasing her wife out of her grumpy-sounding mood. She was also trying hard not to get angry. The two pregnancies had been Allyssa's idea. She only went along with the idea to please her wife. They had both became pregnant, and *now*, she wasn't happy?

"I know. I know," she answered, staring out at the hills and fields on both sides of their driveway. Mentally, she told herself she would have to put in some snow fences this year. She promised herself she would install them last winter and had forgotten.

"What's the matter with you, hon?" She was feeling exasperated with her young wife. They were both pregnant, and there was nothing they could do to change it now. They had wanted this, hadn't they?

"I'm sorry, Fey. I know I should be excited by this, and I am happy." Allyssa stroked her own belly while also looking over at her wife's rounding tummy. "I guess I really didn't think it through, and I'm just shocked that it worked. I mean, what a stereotype…two lesbians pregnant at the same time."

Fey laughed. It *was* a stereotype, but they were the only ones that knew. "Do you want to keep it quiet until you are further along? Technically, you are beyond the first trimester and you could tell people if you wanted." She glanced around at the greening fields and

wondered if their tenant would want to dig up any of them. She couldn't recall her grandparents plowing this far out on the ranch. They'd only farmed around the homestead and out from there.

"Oh, yes. Let's not tell anyone just yet," she answered, a little relieved. She hadn't known that telling people was bothering her at all until Fey asked. "I guess I'm just worried that I'll lose it again like last year."

"Well, it is a little soon to get pregnant again," she pointed out, wishing she had been a little more insistent back in January about waiting, but she had been so relieved when her wife wanted back in their life. She would have given her anything at that moment, including these children they were both carrying. "Your body does need time to heal."

"I have youth on my side," Allyssa quipped and then realized how that sounded. She tried to make amends, "I mean...I don't think..."

"It's okay. I know I'm older," Fey answered. Her feelings were not hurt. She wasn't so old that she couldn't carry a child to term and give birth safely. Still, in her job she had to be very careful. She was relieved the interns would soon be there to help.

"I'm sorry, Fey. I'm not making this easy, am I?" Allyssa asked, feeling like she was being a real shit to her wife. She'd had so much happen to her in the last couple years. She'd grown up a lot, but apparently, she still had some growing to do.

"I worry sometimes, if it is all too much," she answered, her hand gesture taking in the many acres of land before them although a small line of subtle hills was hiding the beauty of their valley from them at that moment.

"You don't think I can cope?" she asked, worrying that Fey was losing confidence in her abilities.

"Well, you have the ranch to run along with the office, the house, and the rescue. You also volunteer with the rehab and the 4-H. And now, you are going to have to raise your baby and mine!"

"Fey, I thought they were *our* babies, not yours or mine?" she asked quietly, sounding much younger than she should.

Fey immediately realized she had misspoken and nodded. "Yes, they are *our* babies but there will be two of them. How will you cope with everything?"

"I know you won't be around all the time because of your job, but you will be there for me and for us," she indicated their two bellies, reaching out to touch Fey's, "when we truly need you. We'll just have

to figure it out. We have time," she said, sounding a little relieved as she pulled her hand back.

"We're having a baby," Fey said softly, wonderingly.

"We're having two babies," Allyssa nearly sobbed, looking in her wife's eyes as Fey caressed her rounding belly. They shared a smile of understanding; glad they had discussed it.

Fey nodded and put the Jeep in gear to drive home. "Hey, didn't you want to shop?" she asked, suddenly remembering.

"You know, I would rather just go home for now," she admitted. "Do you have to go back out?"

"Let's see what's waiting for us both before we make any more plans."

They headed up the drive and when they crested that last hill, they surveyed their little valley containing their new, red, two-story farmhouse with white trim. Their home had been burned down twice, and they had rebuilt it twice. Their huge, wooden barn looked warm and solid, and next to it were corrals that housed a llama, horses, and a donkey. Between the barn and the cabin with an add-on out back was a shed that had been converted to a chicken coop. The chickens were clucking outside the wire after having escaped their pen. In the middle of the ranch yard, creating a natural island in the drive that people drove around, was a fountain in a pool with a statue of a horse in the middle. On the porch of their cabin stood their dog, wagging his tail as he recognized their Jeep.

Next to the cabin, parked in its place of honor, stood an EarthRoamer XV. This was the ultimate RV that they had converted into a mobile vet office for Fey. She was able to work and sleep in this RV for her job. It could keep her going for weeks on the road, if necessary. It was compact, and being solar-powered, it was also energy efficient. It was built to go anywhere with its four-wheel drive and powerful turbo diesel engine. Both women smiled when they saw the pictures of the cartoon characters on the sides of the RV. They were various animals that Fey might have as patients—everything from a rabbit having a belly laugh to a dog scratching its ear in an awkward pose. There was also a cat with a satisfied look (as though it had just eaten a canary) and a cute and cozy-looking lamb. There were so many characters, the effect was almost overwhelming and yet it was also very endearing. The characters were funny and playful and were also great advertising for their business with "HERRIOT VETERINARY SERVICES" stenciled on the door and "Vet-Mobile" and their phone number displayed in smaller letters below their company name. The

back door of the truck cab showed a herd of realistic-looking horses in full gallop.

"I love that RV, baby," Fey mentioned, not for the first time.

"We are lucky, aren't we?" Allyssa agreed, reaching across to squeeze Fey's hand. She mentally resolved not to bum her wife out again with any sad thoughts, fears, or negative thoughts about her own pregnancy. They had so much to do before the babies came and it wouldn't do to upset either of them. She remembered the saying: fake it until you make it, and she resolved she would pretend to be happy until she really *was* happy.

Fey pulled up by the cabin just a bit short of the steps since a chicken was in the way.

"Wanna help me round them up?" Allyssa asked, exasperated with their chickens, who had become such great escape artists.

"Absolutely," Fey agreed, turning off the Jeep and immediately getting out to trap the chicken that had stopped her from pulling up next to the steps. Both their dog on the porch and the other dog that came up to greet her were interested in the fluttering chicken as she grabbed it. "Hello, Rocky," she greeted the Great Dane. "Are your parents here?" she asked as she tucked the chicken under her arm and reached to pet him. He looked down to the barn where their two therapists were working with a child mounted on a horse and wearing a helmet. Woody Franklin and Rhonda Blecher were the therapists renting space on their ranch to work with people on horses as well as rehabilitate the horses Allyssa and Fey had taken in from a rescue.

"Hi there, Rex," Allyssa said to the dog who had laid back down on the porch, his tail thumping against the wood. In fact, Thumper had been his original name for just that reason. Allyssa had accidentally hit him with her car, and later, she not only saved his life but also adopted him. Rex's accident was the reason she had met her wife.

"Hey, Doc, Allyssa," Renee came outside to greet them.

"What's up with the chickens?" Allyssa asked, trying to pick up another that was eyeing her with a definite 'No, you aren't catching me' look.

"They revolted. I swear," she responded, helping to cut off the chicken that would have run from Allyssa.

"Well, if we don't keep 'em safe, the hawks and coyotes will get 'em," she said as she handed the chicken to their assistant and returned to the car to replace her gun on her hip. She had taken to carrying a gun back when they had to run off some rustlers nearly two years ago. It had often come in handy, but today, she had taken it off to go into the

clinic and had forgotten to put it back on. She saw Fey catch another chicken and return it to the coop before heading for the cabin to fetch her own gun. She wore hers for safety as well but not as regularly as Allyssa. Hearing heroic stories of a vet willing to take on rustlers ensured they got a lot of curious calls from people in the area.

After they had the chickens back behind the safety of their fence, Fey went down to talk to Rhonda and Woody. Rex went with Allyssa to the house and then later walked with her down along their fence line to look off into the hills. The view from their little valley was quite spectacular. Far off, they could see the Blue Mountains of Oregon and between the mountains and their newly-built ranch house was a whole lot of high prairie with a mountain-fed lake hidden within it. As Rex snuffled around at the various things along the fence line, Allyssa looked off into the hills that she wanted to explore. Unfortunately, riding was off her 'to do' list until after her pregnancy. Jeez, what had she been thinking? Last year, she had been so happy to be pregnant and now, she was scared. She rubbed her tummy thoughtfully as she stared off into the hills. She saw moving dots that she knew were cattle or horses since they had both on their range. Then, a speck of red caught her eye for a moment.

"Penny for your thoughts?" Fey came up behind her. Rex wagged his tail in greeting but didn't bother to approach the vet. He had serious messages to explore. Rocky, the Great Dane owned by Woody and Rhonda, joined them, and an intense snuffling went on as the two canines exchanged messages.

Allyssa smiled. Fey was her best friend. She'd never had a friend like her before. She was also her wife, her lover, and in a way, her boss. But she was also more of a partner than Allyssa could have ever imagined. "I swear there is something out there," she said, sweeping her hand over the fence towards the plains.

"Always is," Fey agreed, worrying about her wife's mental and physical well-being. She just didn't seem as happy about this pregnancy as Fey. Although both women had attempted to conceive at the same time, they hadn't really believed both would take. "I used to imagine there were ghost horses out there."

"Ghost horses?"

Fey nodded. "When I was growing up, I swear I saw horses that weren't there. Even those mountains sometimes make me see things that aren't there."

"Are you sure they aren't there? Maybe the clouds are just hiding them."

Fey nodded in agreement. "Logically, I know some of the formations aren't there, yet sometimes, I see things when I look out at them. I see things on the range too." She also gestured to the range. "No bringing any ghost horses home," she warned her teasingly. She squinted out on the range, a flash of red catching her eye as she turned to her wife.

Allyssa laughed, as she was intended to. She knew Fey was worried about her lack of enthusiasm, but she was afraid of letting Fey down. As she looked in her wife's brown eyes, she thought about how lucky she was to have met this admirable, brilliant, and beautiful woman. Her wife was not classically beautiful, but she had an aura of self-confidence about her that made Allyssa wish to be a better woman. She smiled and leaned down to kiss her, turning it into a make-out session until they both heard a snort from one of the pens. It was only a horse clearing its nasal passages, but it sounded like a person snorting, "Enough," and they pulled apart, both pleased with their mutual and impromptu display of affection.

"It'll be okay. We'll figure it out," Fey said softly, brushing Allyssa's hair back behind her ear. She loved that the younger woman was taller than her. It felt good, it felt right, and she loved this woman very much. She was just concerned how she would cope with everything they had taken on.

"We will," she said, leaning her head down on Fey's strong shoulder. They could do anything together and had proven it time and again.

TO BE CONTINUED...

Check out all my books at: www.kannemeinel.com.

About the Author

K'Anne Meinel is a Lesbian Fiction bestselling author with more than 100 published works including shorts, novellas, and novels. She is an American author born in Milwaukee, Wisconsin and raised in Oconomowoc. Upon early graduation from high school she went to a private college in Milwaukee and then moved to California for seventeen years before returning to the state. Many of her stories have Wisconsin in them as settings for her wonderful, realistic, and detailed backgrounds. Named the lesbian Danielle Steel of her time, K'Anne continues to write interesting stories in a variety of genres in both the lesbian and mainstream fiction categories.

~ Because a publisher should stand behind their authors~

What do you do when you meet someone who changes everything you know about love and passion?

Paige Harlow is a good girl. She's always known where she was going in life: top grades, an ivy league school, a medical degree, regular church attendance, and a happy marriage to a man. So falling in love with her gorgeous roommate and best friend Alyssa Torres is no small crisis. Alyssa is chasing demons of her own, a medical condition that makes her an outcast and a family dysfunctional to the point of disintegration make her a questionable choice for any stable relationship. But Paige's heart is no longer her own. She must now battle the prejudices of her family, friends, and church and come to peace with her new sexuality before she can hope to win the affections of the woman of her dreams. But will love be enough?

www.shadoepublishing.com

~ Because a publisher should stand behind their authors~

When Delaney Delacroix is called to locate a missing girl, she never plans on getting caught up with a human trafficking investigation or with the local witch. Meeting with Raelin Montrose changes her life in so many ways that Delaney isn't sure that this isn't destiny.

Raelin Montrose is a practicing Wiccan, and when the ley lines that run under her home tell her that someone is coming, she can't imagine that she was going to solve a mystery and find the love of her life at the same time.

~ Because a publisher should stand behind their authors~

Amelia Gittens had the credit of being the first and only woman thus far in the United States military of being a sniper in combat, made possible by being in the Military Police unit of the crack 10th Mountain Infantry Division. After retirement she joins the City of New York Police Department, and suddenly finds herself involved in a suspect shooting incident which soon encroaches upon her entire life. In order to protect her therapist who has been targeted as a revenge killing, Amelia takes on the responsibility as if she was still in the Army, treating it as a tactical maneuver.

~ Because a publisher should stand behind their authors~

An abused and bullied teenager is suddenly granted great and terrible powers by an ancient goddess. Each step towards womanhood is shaped by her new abilities, as is the woman she will become. Devil or angel, which will she be? Will the woman who chases her ever know for sure?

Both men tried to shoot her then, and the two women were stunned at the speed with which she moved. Penny charged straight at the gunmen then dove under their fire. Spinning on her back she kicked the legs from under one man, and as he fell, she kicked the gun from the other man's hand. Spinning back to the first man she saw the gun barrel moving toward her, and she lashed out with her foot. Her boot crushed his skull and she rolled to her feet to grab the last man in a neck lock. A quick twist and he lay lifeless in her arms.

She let him fall, as, breathing deeply, she came down off combat mode. "Are you ladies all right?" she asked as she untied the ropes that held the older woman.

"Who are you?" asked the old woman fearfully, as she pulled the tape from her mouth.

"They call me Lady Blue," smiled Penny as she helped the woman to stand.

"What are you?" It was the younger woman who spoke.

"Cold, hungry, dead tired, and covered in blue war paint," giggled Penny as she released the older woman's arm. She turned and began to search the bodies.